ALL the Fields

Christopher Valen

This book is a work of fiction. Names, characters, places and incidents either are products of the author's imagination or are used fictitiously. Any resemblance to actual events, or to actual persons living or dead, is entirely coincidental.

ALL THE FIELDS

Cover Design: Rebecca Treadway

Books by Christopher Valen

The John Santana Series

White Tombs
The Black Minute
Bad Weeds Never Die
Bone Shadows
Death's Way
The Darkness Hunter
Speak for the Dead

It's all I have to bring today—
This, and my heart beside—
This, and my heart, and all the fields—
And all the meadows wide—

Emily Dickinson

Prologue

The seasons of baseball have always divided my life. Instead of fairy tales, I knew of Nolan Ryan, Bert Blyleven, Greg Maddux, and Tom Glavin. Before I learned to walk, my father had given me my first glove, and by the time I was twenty-one, a New York Mets' scout had signed me after I pitched my last game for the University of Minnesota. We had won the conference title and made it all the way to Omaha and the College World Series before Arizona eliminated us. I won fifteen games that year, including a three-hitter against Texas in the first round of the series.

Fond memories of Virginia and my last year in professional baseball with the Mets' Triple-A club in Norfolk stay with me like a sweet dream. I remember the wild ponies on Assateague Island, bream and bluegill in the freshwater ponds and streams, flounder and sea trout in the tidal waters, and oyster and scallops in Chesapeake Bay. I remember how the sun flamed the horizon orange as it set over the Blue Ridge Mountains, and how the mist settled like cotton over the Shenandoah Valley at dawn. I remember walking the streets in the cities of Richmond and Williamsburg, the towns of Marion and Lynchburg, recalling the first heartbeat of a nation. I was a hot property at the time, one step away from the majors.

When I put my name on my first professional contract, my father was there in the locker room with me. So were my teammates, my college coach, Paul Tatum, and reporters from the press and TV.

"A dream come true," my father said.

Growing up in a small town among fields of wheat, he'd had dreams of his own. Vietnam had interrupted those dreams, and a piece of shrapnel, which had lodged in his throwing arm, had ended them.

I didn't know then how much my success meant to my father. Often he would come home from work exhausted and still find the energy to practice with me for hours at a time. Serious and demanding, he accepted nothing less than my best effort. I found it tough not to comply. How could I not give my all when he gave me everything he had?

For the gift of competitiveness, I am eternally grateful. But from him I also learned to seek praise instead of affection, always trying to please, putting undue pressure on myself. And though he never physically abused me, when he withheld that praise, used it as a weapon, it hurt me as much as any beating I could have suffered.

My father met my mother a dozen years after returning from Vietnam. They moved into a house in Oak Grove, a suburb of Minneapolis, one of the thousands of suburbs that mushroomed throughout the country in the housing explosion of the fifties and sixties.

A year after my parents bought the house, my brother, Rick, was born. I arrived two years later. The delivery was long and difficult; my mother could not have another child, never have the daughter she always wanted, so ours was a household of boys, of scratches and scrapes, of Band-Aids and grass stains. Meals were timed to coincide with the ends of practices and games, the food often kept warm until seven or eight in the evening. I can't ever remember a time when my mother complained, or a time when I wasn't playing ball.

Blessed with a dark beauty and an uncanny eye for details, my mother was our umpire. An avid reader not only of books but also of people, she was able to see the curves, detect the subtle changes in the rhythm and flow of life. She mediated disputes, settled arguments, allowed our childhood to play itself out as if it were one long, endless summer game, each moment an inning, each inning another year to be savored and remembered.

She made certain we never went to school hungry or with torn or dirty clothes, and—though we never had much money—she always found enough for that new glove or shiny pair of spikes. I recall days when the aroma of apple pie filled the house; how she used to bake extra strips of dough and sprinkle cinnamon on them. At night she often opened the family scrapbook and told us stories about my grandfather, my namesake, Michael Collins, a pitcher so feared for his blazing fastball that even today his name is mentioned with reverence in town leagues throughout the state. From my mother I developed a love of stories and a dreamer's spirit, a spirit that was easily wounded in the skirmishes of life.

Before we were old enough for organized leagues, my father hung an old tire from the oak tree in our backyard, and I would spend hours trying to throw balls through its center. Each evening in the summer, after dinner, he would take Rick and me to the field across the street, where we would throw and catch until dark.

It seemed natural that my brother, Rick, would become a catcher. Shorter and stockier than me, with my father's blond hair and complexion, he had a catcher's physique and temperament. Besides, I was left-handed and, in the beginning, too small to catch my big brother's throws. Later, as I grew taller and stronger and could get some leverage on my fastball, one could hear the pop of baseball against leather in the quiet of the neighborhood at dusk as I hummed fastball after fastball into Rick's mitt.

My brother was serious and thoughtful, slow to anger, willing to take the everyday bumps and bruises a catcher had to endure without so much as a whimper. Once, in Little League, when a foul tip left the bone protruding grotesquely from his index finger, he calmly walked over to the coach and told him someone would have to catch the next inning while he got his finger splinted. Even as he held his broken finger out to the coach and his teammates gagged, Rick blinked back the tears. He was more like Dad in that respect, keeping his feelings hidden, no matter how painful.

When I was twelve, my father was driving a semi from coast to coast, trying to keep his fledging trucking firm afloat. In the winter he would often be gone for weeks. It was on one of those rare occasions when he was home, the night after he had returned from a two-week trip, that I awoke to voices. It was two o'clock in the morning.

I got out of bed and wandered into the hallway, walking barefoot across the soft carpet to the iron railing at the head of the stairs, dressed in my pajamas, my eyes gradually adjusting to the light. I stood listening for a time, concentrating, hearing little of what was being said, noting only that the tone was serious. I wanted to get closer even if it meant that I might be seen.

Heart thumping, I descended the stairs that led down to the dining room, taking care to avoid the creak in the loose board on the third step from the bottom. From there I inched along the wall to my left until I came to the kitchen door, always slightly ajar because it sat crooked on its hinges. I could see clearly through the crack between the doorjamb and door. The two of them were sitting at the kitchen table; my mother's voice was soothing.

"It's going to be okay, hon."

"It's no use. We just can't save enough to get the business off the ground."

"Give it a little more time," she said. "I know it's what you want."

There was a momentary silence. Worried that they knew I was listening, I considered making my way quickly up the stairs to my room, but my feet felt too heavy to move.

Then my father said, "You want to know what I think sometimes, Rose? Sometimes when I'm driving along some country road in the middle of nowhere? I think about never coming back. I really think about it. I hate myself for it, but it's true."

I saw my mother get up and put her arms around his head, drawing him to her breast as she would a child. "We're going to make it, Carl. You'll see." And then I heard something that I had never heard before, something that I never heard again. I heard my father cry.

In that instant, tears brimming in my own eyes, I ran into the kitchen and threw my arms around his neck. I told him how much I loved him; how I would always be good, always do my best, always do what he wanted, if he promised he would never go away.

I remember his look of utter astonishment and then his smile, which seemed to work its way through his tears. Embracing me in his thick arms, he said, "Don't worry, son. I'm not going anywhere."

My father kept his word.

I didn't.

Perhaps if I hadn't met Laura, things could have been different between us. I don't know.

Chapter 1

Dust mites suspended above the bar tables mute the late afternoon sunlight, which filters through unwashed windows, creating the illusion that it is much later in the day. It is, in fact, four-thirty on a Friday afternoon, and I'm nearly drunk. I received my termination notice an hour ago.

"I'd better call Pam," I say to Mac Tyler and Kate Fleming, who sit on bar stools on each side of me, "before the screwdrivers go to work on my brain cells."

Mac nods and finishes off his mug of beer. "I'll order us another round."

"Not for me," Kate says. "I've reached my limit." She smiles, runs a hand through her thick red hair, and stands up.

"Katie, Katie," Mac says, imitating an Irish brogue. "Mike and I have only just begun. I do believe you're slowing down in your advancing age."

Mac and I always tell Kate how much she reminds us of Maureen O'Hara in movies like *The Quiet Man* with John Wayne. She has Maureen's look and fiery demeanor.

"Never," she laughs. "I promised my husband I'd cook dinner tonight. It's my turn."

"Will we see you at Jack Stone's party tomorrow night?" I ask.

"Wouldn't miss it." She reaches out and touches me gently on the shoulder. "I'm sorry you lost your job, Michael. I wish you could have mine."

"Thanks, Kate. I appreciate it."

She waves at us both, smiles, and heads for the door.

I pull out my cell phone. My head is light and my stomach full. Waylon Jennings' voice coming from the jukebox across the room warns: "Mamas, don't let your babies grow up to be cowboys."

Waylon could have said the same thing about schoolteachers.

The malt smell of spilled beer hangs in the stale air. Around me, men with day-old beards, thick, tattooed arms, and oily baseball hats with PETERBILT stitched across the front sit at small wooden tables. They're drinking boilermakers and complaining about the state of the country.

"I'm at Sammy's," I say to Pam when she answers.

"Is something the matter, Michael? You sound different."

"You mean drunk."

"No," she says. "I mean different. I thought we were going out for dinner."

"Meet me for a drink first."

There's a pause.

"All right. But I wish you'd tell me what's wrong."

"What could be wrong? It's happy hour."

As I disconnect, I recall the dartboard that I have in my room at school. Actually, it isn't a dartboard. A student drew a target on the chalkboard one day when I was absent and the sub was out of the room. I left the target on the board. Each day I tape a new vocabulary word in the center, hoping to generate some class discussion. I call it the target word for the day. I think of myself now as a dart flung through the air by the hand of fate; a dart that has landed way off center.

"You know, Mac, maybe I should stick the word TERMINATE on my chalkboard next Monday. If I use the word SHAFT, we'll end up talking about drive shafts and crankshafts."

"Shaft is what you got, all right," Mac says, resting one of his size twelve cowboy boots on the boot rail.

Mac Tyler teaches the "burnouts" in the room across the hall from me at Woodrow Wilson High School. He wears a T-shirt with the sleeves cut off at the shoulder and a pair of soiled blue jeans. *SEMPER FI* is tattooed on his right forearm. His leather jacket is draped over the stool beside him. Mac has great success with troubled kids because he was one himself. I wonder why I've had such success with special education kids.

"I guess that leaves just you and Kate Fleming in the special education department, Mac, now that Beth Stanton and I have been cut."

"I can't see Kate retiring for a few years."

"Or you either."

Mac grins. "Not if my wife has anything to say about it." He drinks from his mug of beer.

I envy the freedom Mac has in his classroom. Rarely does he have to worry about the administration looking over his shoulder. He practically has to threaten them before they'll set foot in his classroom.

"Hey, they've got to start hiring pretty soon, Mike. The statistics say there's a teacher shortage coming. Just hang in there."

A female bartender wearing Levi's and a tank top brings me another screwdriver and Mac another beer. Her tennis shoes crunch the peanut shells that are scattered on the floor. Outside of a popcorn machine and a bin of salted-in-the-shell peanuts, Sammy's has very few frills and even less chic. No plants and no exposed pipes, except for the lead one Sammy keeps under the counter behind the bar.

"School's out next week, Mac. I've got no money saved, a 2005 Chevy that barely runs, and no prospects for future employment. And I've accomplished all this in twenty-eight years."

"I got some friends who own a cycle shop. Summer's a busy time. You need a job to tide you over, let me know. I'll give 'em a call."

"Thanks. But I might just rest on my laurels."

"You know," Mac says, stroking the hair in his dark, shaggy beard, "you were just in the wrong place at the wrong time, my friend."

"That's the story of my life."

* * *

Pam sits across the table from me, unbuttoning the tailored blue suit jacket that she wears over her white silk blouse. Her brown hair matches the color of her eyes. We're at a restaurant that features lots of stained glass, potted plants, dark wood, and polished brass. The after-work crowd is three deep at the bar, rubbing shoulders and whatever else. The noise level is a little less than if we were dining on a runway. Carrying on a conversation takes some effort, an effort that only Pam chooses to make.

She's saying something about the possibility of an upcoming promotion at the bank. I keep smiling at what I think are appropriate times, but I'm really not listening. Instead I'm thinking, *Why don't I love this woman*? Pam is nice looking. She has a nice figure, a nice personality. My friends and family think she's nice. Sex is nice. Everything is nice; so nice that it's driving me crazy. Just once I want Pam to swear. I'm not sure why, and yet I'd probably be upset if she did.

We've been dating for seven months now, or is it eight? She often sends me cards, nice cards with cute sayings. I read them and then recycle them.

I gave Pam a humorous card on her twenty-seventh birthday. If I'd given her a sentimental, romantic card, the kind that I used to buy Laura, Pam might have gotten the wrong idea. She might think that I care about her more than I do. That would be a lie. And though I've lied to her about some things, I draw the line when it comes to lying about love.

"If I get this promotion, Michael, I'm going to sell my condo."

I nod my head. It's the first thing I've heard clearly in the last five minutes. I'm wondering what I'm going to do with the rest of my life. I can't go on like this much longer.

"I'd like to get a bigger place," Pam continues. "In case . . ."

I know what she's thinking. She launches into it every date like a ship on the open sea. I know every harbor, every tide, every current along the way, and I know the exact moment that her conclusion will steam into port. I need to change the subject.

"I'll order more wine."

"None for me, Michael. I'm fine."

I motion for the waitress.

Pam asks if I want the last of the appetizers, a potato skin covered with cheese and bacon.

"No, thanks." I'm having trouble focusing. I'm not sure how we got to the restaurant. Then I remember. The thought that I actually drove drunk sends a shiver through me. The thought that Pam let me drive makes me angry. But she lets me do a lot of things. She's just that way.

"Would you like to split it?" she asks, pointing to the lone potato skin.

"No, Pam. You eat it. Please."

Certain things about her irritate me, like the fine, dark line just above her upper lip. The way she walks. Fast. Determined. Swinging her arms as if to propel her body forward. Not graceful. Not sexy.

She snores. Last weekend her snoring woke me. I left her bed and went to the living room couch. When she found me there, I felt like a jerk. I didn't want to tell her that she snored, so I lied and said that I couldn't sleep.

A waitress brings our dinners. I ordered chicken Kiev, Pam the same.

"Could you bring me another glass of white wine?" I say.

"Of course."

Trying not to appear conspicuous, I watch the waitress walk away, enthralled by the sway of her hips.

"How's your chicken, Michael? Michael?"

"Huh?" I say, looking at Pam again.

"You seem preoccupied."

I want to say I'm preoccupied with holding up my head, but instead I blurt, "I got my final termination notice today."

"Oh, no." Pam clasps a hand over her mouth.

I hadn't planned on telling her yet. The words just came out. It reminds me of the times when I stayed up too late, on the edge of sleep, and tried carrying on a conversation. Sometimes the sound of my voice startles me, and I don't realize what I've said till after I've said it.

"It's a rite of spring, Pam. The snow melts, robins return, I get my termination notice."

"I'm sorry. What are you going to do?" She slides a hand across the table and touches mine.

I pull away. Then, embarrassed, I pick up my half-empty wine glass and make a toast. "I'm doing it."

"I knew there was something wrong. I just knew it."

"How did you know?"

"I know you, Michael."

"No you don't."

She sits back in her chair, only the sudden color in her complexion betraying her feelings.

I finish off my wine and eat a bite of chicken.

"I don't blame you for being angry, Michael. It's not fair that you keep losing your job. You're a good teacher."

"How do you know I'm a good teacher? Have you ever seen me teach?"

She doesn't answer. She just sits there watching me, her cheeks flushed.

I focus my eyes on the chicken.

The waitress comes by with more wine and takes away my empty glass.

Pam says, "There's something else, Michael, isn't there."

I keep staring at the chicken, thinking how appropriate an order it is. I know I've been kidding myself. She isn't Laura. I have to tell her. I have to tell her that I don't love her and that I never will. I've rehearsed the dialogue so many times that I can recite it by heart. *I'm sorry, Pam, but I don't love you. It's not your fault.*

I'm reminded of the *Seinfeld* episode in which George's girlfriend breaks up with him by saying, "It's not you, it's me." George is offended, as he considers this to be his signature break-up line.

"There's something else, isn't there?" Pam says again.

I start to say, "Yes," then recover and attempt to say, "No." What comes out of my mouth is a sliver of chicken and a word that sounds slightly Russian. The sliver of chicken lands on Pam's white silk blouse.

"I'm sorry."

I pick up my napkin and reach across the table to brush off her blouse. In the process I knock over my glass of wine. It spills in her lap. I wait for her to say what I'm thinking. *Shit!*

"It's okay," she says.

The couple sitting at the table next to us is staring as if they have never spilled anything in their lives.

"What are you looking at?" I say.

A waitress rushes over to our table with a bar rag the size of a sail. Pam excuses herself and heads for the ladies' room.

Though the restaurant is air conditioned, sweat runs down my back, and the inside of my head roars as if my ears are pressed against seashells. I realize quite suddenly that my fingers and toes are tingling, and I have trouble catching my breath, and I know I have to get out of here before I start hyperventilating.

I stand and bolt toward the door.

Outside, the night air feels fresh and clean. A breeze cools my back. I move toward my car, at least toward where I think my car is. There are more cars in the lot now, and I'm confused. I seem to be walking slightly off the ground. I realize that Pam might never forgive me for leaving her here, that it's a lousy thing to do—but I don't go back.

Three women walk by me. As they pass, I catch the sweet scent of lilac.

I remember how my heart used to skip when I was with someone special, how it used to skip when I looked at Laura. I remember how I made her laugh. I was funnier then. There's less to laugh about now.

I watch the three women as they enter the restaurant. I smile, though my eyes blur with tears. I can't see, can't feel my legs. I move in slow motion. Fighting off the urge to cry, I keep smiling. I don't know why I feel like crying, or why I continue to smile.

I don't know why I do anything.

Chapter 2

On Saturday night I drive through downtown Dakota Lake with its narrow streets and small specialty shops with names like Country Quilt and Wicks and Sticks. I drive by the weathered frame houses and summer cottages along the south side of the lake, past the larger homes and eighteen-hole golf course on my left and the private yacht club on my right.

The southern half of town, nearest the yacht club, has its own modern high school, Seaton, named after the former mayor and wealthiest family in Dakota Lake. Alexander Seaton lives with his third wife on Gull Island in the middle of the lake, reachable only by ferryboat in summer and snowmobile in winter. I went to the island just once to see Alexander Seaton, yet I feel our lives are inexorably linked, as if we're the sole survivors of some unspeakable catastrophe.

Seaton's great-grandfather was one of the founders of the town back in the 1850s, when abundant wild game and lakes left by retreating glaciers first attracted settlers to this area. This attraction continued well into the 1900s as streetcars brought vacationers out to the lake from the city. The town soon became known as a resort community; a reputation the city council continues to encourage, despite a lack of commercial development.

I teach at Wilson High School north of town, near the trailer courts and HUD developments.

The citizens on the north side have lobbied the school board for the past few years to raze Wilson and build an addition onto Seaton High so that all the students in Dakota Lake can attend the same modern high school. But money and power increase the closer you live to the yacht club. Not until recently, when new housing developments began to grow the population of the north side and the balance on the board shifted, did those favoring the razing of Wilson High finally prevail.

The town has a schizophrenic personality, perpetuated by gossip, rumors and outright delusions, which have developed into bitter community rivalries over the years. Wilson has dominated in football and hockey, Seaton in basketball and baseball. Wilson's faculty is noted for its fine chemistry, science and math programs, while Seaton excels in literature, history and debate.

I park my Chevy in front of Jack Stone's house. Jack is the principal of Woodrow Wilson High School, and tonight is the annual spring faculty party. Last September I attended the annual fall faculty party, also at Jack Stone's house. My spirits were higher then, and I had a glassy-eyed naiveté usually found only in first-year teachers. That night I drank little, laughed at all the appropriate times, tried to appear interested in mundane conversation. Many of my colleagues were impressed.

So was Jack Stone's wife, Nicole.

Last fall seems like years ago. I'm not the same person now; something besides my job has changed—or maybe something has been changing for a long time, and I finally noticed. I considered skipping the spring party at the Stones' house. I told myself it was because I'd received my termination notice, and that I would feel out of place. But feeling out of place was nothing new. I had a better reason for skipping the party.

The Stones' large colonial sits on a hill across from Ridgewood Park and Dakota Lake. Like a stuffy aristocrat, it competes with the Tudor, Spanish and Georgian style residences for the best view of the lake. When I found out that Nicole's family had money, I understood how she and Jack could afford to live here.

Sailboats dot the water like mushrooms on a sea of grass. A water skier clings to an invisible towrope behind a speedboat, following it as if guided by radar. Joggers hurry along the asphalt path that winds around the lake, and near the grassy shoreline an old man tosses slices of white bread into a gaggle of honking geese. A man and a woman sit on a wooden bench holding hands, oblivious to the activity around them, as a breath of clover drifts in the warm evening air.

My eyes burn as I think of Laura and how we used to walk together around this lake. For just a moment I see the two of us walking through shimmering heat mirages. The thought causes a familiar ache in my chest, and the memories come flooding in. I take two deep breaths till the feeling passes.

As I walk across the Stones' expansive lawn, the thick, rich color of the grass reminds me of a baseball diamond. I follow the sidewalk that leads around the house to the backyard, where I hear voices and the sound of Mozart on the stereo. I figure I'll make an early appearance, and then, when the crowd shows up and it's less conspicuous, a quiet exit.

One of Jack Stone's hobbies is carpentry, and recently he added a deck to the back of his house. A half dozen of Wilson's staff members are gathered there. I know their names but little else about them.

Why bother? I won't be back next year anyway.

I see myself as an actor reprising a role in a recurring play. It seems that no matter where the play is performed and with whom, the ending is always the same.

Bob Haber, the assistant principal, waves "Hello." Tall and gaunt, Bob took up speed walking last fall to lose weight. In his polo shirt and shorts, he looks like a concentration camp survivor.

Jack Stone, lighting coals on a large gas grill, gives me a nod. Jack wears a chef's hat, which covers his bald head, and an apron that reads NUMBER ONE CHEF. An ex-Marine fighter pilot, Jack is six feet two and looks as if he spends hours in the weight room, which he doesn't. Jack doesn't like kids very much. It surprises me that he's principal of a high school. But

Jack's degree is in business administration, and I imagine he planned to remain business manager of the district till some board member—who hadn't been in a high school in twenty years—decided that he would make a great principal.

In the late eighties, Jack was known as "Stonebreaker" when he played halfback for Michigan. Privately, he's still called that by many of the students and staff at Wilson.

"Good to see you, Collins," he says, shaking my hand. The strength of his grip catches me by surprise. "There's beer in the fridge and hors d'oeuvres on the dining room table. Help yourself."

I keep stretching and relaxing my hand as I slide open the patio screen and step through the French doors and into the living room. I wonder if Jack deliberately tried to hurt me, or if he's already had too much to drink and just misjudged his strength. Rumors of Jack's drinking have been whispered in the teacher's lounge. Staff members wonder if the pressures of the job are finally getting to Jack. I never wonder. I know exactly what Jack's problem is.

Inside the house, Beth Stanton comes up to me with a resigned look and says, "Too bad, eh?" Beth's ash blonde hair is long and straight like her figure. "You know, Michael, I'm only twenty-two, and this is my first teaching assignment and termination notice. So I guess I don't feel as bad as you. I mean, you're almost thirty. It must be awful to keep losing your teaching position year after year."

"Thanks for reminding me."

"Sorry. But you'll find another job. Just keep applying."

Beth means well. She just has a habit of saying the wrong thing at the wrong time. Excusing myself, I head for the kitchen and a cold beer.

As I hold open the refrigerator door and reach for a can of Coors, a voice behind me says, "Why haven't you called me, Michael?"

If there were enough room to crawl inside the refrigerator, I would have. It isn't that Nicole Stone is hard to look at. Her prominent cheekbones and smooth complexion suggest she is at least ten years younger than forty-four. But she reminds me of some of the models I see in retail catalogues. They have a cold beauty about them; perfection that makes them appear elusive, untouchable. Nicole is like that. Even when I was inside her, I never actually touched her.

I grab a cold beer out of the refrigerator and close the door as I turn around to face her. "Hello, Mrs. Stone," I say, looking around to see if we're alone.

She stands so close to me that not even the heavy scent of her Opium perfume masks the smell of Scotch on her breath.

"You knew Jack was at a workshop in Duluth for two days, Michael. I've been all alone."

Nicole's eyes are more gray than blue, like the color of the sky on a windswept November afternoon. Her outfit matches her eyes, and though she probably thinks the silk blouse and jewelry are understated, she appears overdressed.

I pop open the tab on the can, and a little spray of beer hits me in the face. Nicole steps back and touches her hair, making sure every blond strand is in its proper place. I remember how stiff her hair felt the first time it brushed against my cheek.

"Well?" she says.

"I've been busy. I've had a lot on my mind."

"Jack mentioned you weren't going to be rehired. I'm sorry."

"I'll bet Jack's not."

"What's that supposed to mean?"

I swallow a sip of beer. "I think he knows about us."

"Impossible."

"Why is that so impossible?"

"In Jack's wildest imagination, he'd never think that I'd fall for you."

"Thanks for the compliment."

She moves closer to me and places a hand on my sleeve. "I didn't mean it the way it sounded."

Mac Tyler ambles into the kitchen dressed in his familiar ensemble: faded jeans, cut-off T-shirt, and cowboy boots. "Mike," he says with a nod. "Mrs. Stone."

Nicole's complexion flames red. She jerks her hand off my arm and steps back from me. "Nice to see you again," she replies, giving Mac a tight smile.

Nicole once told me that Mac Tyler was the sorriest example of a professional she had ever seen. I wondered what she would think if she knew that Mac had graduated Phi Beta Kappa from the University of Minnesota. But I figure, what the hell? It really doesn't matter what she thinks.

"If you two will excuse me," Nicole says, but in a much lighter tone. She walks out of the kitchen. Her movements appear casual, but like a cat, everything is measured, controlled.

"Lucky it was me who walked in instead of Jack," Mac says.

I trust Mac more than anyone. I know that whatever I tell him won't be tomorrow's gossip in the teacher's lounge. I also know that it was a mistake to get involved with Nicole Stone.

"Is she as cold as she seems?" Mac says nonchalantly, as if he were asking the score of the Twins game.

"No, she's not."

We walk into the dining room to a long table covered with a white linen tablecloth, bowls of salad, plates of fancy-looking hors d'oeuvres, and grilled hamburgers. Light reflects off the crystal chandelier, and the sharp smell of charcoal wafts through the screens.

"You bring your wife, Mac?" I ask.

"The baby's sick. We couldn't get a sitter."

I pick up a china plate and put a hamburger on it. "*Nouveau riche*. Kate Fleming will get a kick out of this."

"I haven't seen her," Mac replies.

"I hope she shows up soon. Kate's always the life of the party."

Mac smiles. "How'd your date with Pam go?"

"Don't ask."

"Too late," he said, loading up a plate with crackers, cheese and dip.

It bothers me that I left Pam at the restaurant, but it bothers me more that sooner or later I'll have to face her. "You ever feel like the world is falling apart around you, Mac?"

"Once," he replies, scooping a tablespoon of potato salad onto his plate. "But sometimes things have to fall apart before you can put them back together."

Jack Stone turns on a floodlight over the garage as Mac and I walk out onto the patio, and the deck lights up like a stage. Hamburgers sizzle on the grill. The smell of fresh cut grass lingers like incense in the air.

Between sips of beer and bites of hamburger, I make idle conversation with the emaciated assistant principal, Bob Haber, and fight off mosquitoes not dissuaded by the smoke from the citronella pails Jack has set up around the deck.

"Not eating, Bob?"

"Only carbos. I've got a race coming up tomorrow. Got to watch the diet. Throwing up all over yourself is no fun."

"I'll bet. Been racing much?"

"Hard to find a good one. Race walking isn't as popular as running. But it's growing. I think as the population ages, more people will get into it." Grinning, he pats his stomach. "I feel like I'm on the cutting edge of a new craze."

"That's great," I say, moving toward Mac.

More staff has arrived, and they're congregated in groups, organized by sex, department, political persuasion, and marital status. I belong to the smallest group in the school: the single, special education department, liberal males.

Ned Fowler, the bull-necked football coach, huddles with Jack. Ned's team finished first in the conference last fall and made it all the way to the semifinals in the playoffs for the state championship.

They're discussing the situation in the Middle East. *Discussing* is the wrong word. With Jack there are no discussions. He tells Ned that we ought to go over there and "kick ass." Jack's voice has become progressively louder in direct proportion to the amount of alcohol he's consumed.

It's about time to make my exit. If I stay here any longer, it'll be difficult to avoid Nicole. I'm considering asking Mac if he wants to get a drink somewhere else when Jack Stone says, "What do you think about Iraq, Collins?"

My cheeks feel sunburned. I shrug. "Haven't given it much thought, Jack."

"You damn well should," he said, slurring his words. "Isn't that right, Mac?"

Jack's got to know I'm sleeping with his wife.

"Give it a rest, Jack," Mac says. He nudges me with his arm. "Let's get a refill."

"Hey!" Jack says as I turn away. I feel the weight of everyone's eyes on me.

Nicole comes out of the house, and my gaze meets hers for an instant. Then she walks over to Jack and whispers something to him.

Jesus, I think. *She didn't.*

"My God!" Jack says loudly.

As a hush settles over the gathering, two scenarios flash in my mind. In one, I'm standing in front of the entire staff at Wilson, apologizing for having slept with the principal's wife while the superintendent intones, "You'll never teach again, Collins." In the second scenario, Jack is beating the shit out of me.

Jack bangs a spatula against the grill till he has everyone's attention. "Nicole just received a phone call from John Fleming, Kate's husband," he says in a voice that suddenly sounds very sober. "I'm afraid there's been an accident."

I hear quick intakes of breath as Jack pauses. I can't believe that I thought Nicole was actually going to say something to Jack about our affair. I must be losing my mind.

"Kate's been rushed to the emergency room at Regions Hospital," Jack continues.

Mac holds his fork full of potato salad halfway between his plate and mouth and looks at me. He doesn't say anything, but he doesn't have to.

If Kate Fleming is injured too severely to continue teaching, or—my God, I don't want to think about it—if she dies, then there'll be a position open in the special education department at Wilson. On paper, I figure I have a better shot at the job than Beth Stanton. But not if Jack Stone finds out that I'm sleeping with his wife.

Chapter 3

Warm wind blows through the open car windows. Over the hood, heat lightning flashes on the far horizon. The speedometer reads fifty, and the chassis on my Chevy begins to sway like a ship in a turbulent sea. The car has nearly reached its limit, and I let up on the accelerator. It's just as well since sometimes I think of steering into the nearest bridge abutment.

It's ten o'clock. A half hour ago I left the Stones' party feeling battered by conflicting emotions, ranging from sadness because Kate was in an accident, to guilt because I want her to be injured seriously enough so that she'll retire from teaching—but not seriously enough that she'll die—to anger because my affair with Nicole Stone could cost me my chance at a permanent teaching position. The line between my personal and professional life has become blurred, as if I'm looking out a window during a rainstorm.

I remember the night I visited the Stones' house back in late October, when the last of the sunburned leaves were hanging for dear life on the trees. I went there to get my briefcase, which Jack had found in the teachers' lounge and brought home. The briefcase contained tests and papers that needed grading for class the next day, so I was relieved when Nicole Stone called. At the time I wondered why she'd waited till evening, after Jack left for his Tuesday night poker game, to call me. But later, driving to the house along damp streets that glistened in the headlights, I'd dismissed the thought.

* * *

"Would you care for a drink, Michael? You don't mind if I call you Michael, do you?"

It wasn't really a question. Besides, what could I say to the principal's wife, a woman who was older than me?

"No, I don't mind." I wasn't about to start calling her Nicole unless she asked. And even then, I'd have to think about it.

She smiled. "Why don't you sit down?"

"I just stopped by to pick up my briefcase."

"The least you can do is tell me something about yourself. We didn't have much of a chance to chat at the fall faculty party."

For an instant, I thought she was interested in more than my life history. *But that's absurd. She's only being polite, trying to make a new teacher feel comfortable, welcome.*

"Let me take your coat," she said.

I slipped out of my leather jacket and handed it to her. She put it on a hanger in the hall closet and gestured toward the living room. "Please, Michael, sit down."

The cushions on the couch were as hard as one of the white bricks in the mantelpiece. The pearl gray carpet was plush, the tables glass-topped with chrome legs, and the walls and upholstered furniture were white, sterile. Everything was expensive, but nothing was personal. I felt as if I was sitting in a showcase.

"What would you like to drink?" she asked as a damp log sizzled in the fireplace grate.

"I'll take a beer if you have one." I noticed the way she moved as she went to the kitchen and returned with a cocktail glass in one hand and a can of Coors in the other. She didn't walk so much as she swayed, like a bough in the wind.

"Here you are," she said with a smile. Her perfume hung in the air like ozone during a storm.

"Thank you." Her light blue sweater and skirt accentuated her blond hair and creamy skin. She struck me as someone who'd never wear jeans and a sweatshirt, even if a designer made them.

She slipped a CD in the Bose system and sat on the love seat across from me, right leg twined over the left, her right shoe dangling from her toe. "So," she said in a low voice, "tell me something about yourself."

I told her a little about college, about signing with the Mets' organization after I graduated, about pitching in the minors for a while and then hanging it up.

She leaned forward with one elbow on her knee. "Are you ever sorry you quit baseball?"

"I don't think about it much."

"Why teaching?"

"It's really the only other thing I know how to do."

She smiled. "What about your wife? What does she do?"

"I'm not married."

"Never?"

I shook my head and drank some beer.

"How did you manage that?"

"Just lucky, I guess," I replied, trying to lighten the conversation.

"You don't believe in marriage?"

"I thought seriously about it. Once."

She tilted her head as if waiting for me to explain.

"It didn't work out."

"Oh," she replied, swirling the ice in her cocktail glass.

Talking like this with her made me uneasy. "What about you?" I asked, wanting to shift the focus of the discussion.

She told me how she'd grown up in Grosse Point, Michigan. Her father was an executive with GM. She'd gone to the University of Michigan and majored in fashion. She'd wanted to become a designer and open her own shop in New York or Paris after graduation, but then she'd met Jack.

I couldn't help but hear the regret in her voice.

"Isn't that interesting, Michael? We're both doing something much different than we thought we would be doing." Her gaze was distant and inward.

The silence that followed was only momentary, but it seemed uncomfortably long.

"Would you like to see the rest of the house?" she said abruptly, focusing her attention on me again. "I've been redecorating."

I quickly drank the last of my beer. "I really should be going soon. I have papers to grade before tomorrow."

"Could you indulge me a moment more?"

Outside, the wind was gusting. I heard it whine in the chimney and felt a draft. I shrugged. "I guess I have a little more time."

"Good."

I trailed behind her, trying to appear interested as she described in great detail what she'd done or was about to do to each room in the house. But mostly I watched her. A couple of times she turned around quickly, as if sensing she was being watched, and I had to pretend that I was looking at something else. Upstairs, we walked down a hallway, past a closed door, and I wondered what was in there, why she didn't show me.

"This is my room," she said when we reached the master bedroom at the end of the hall. She flicked on the light switch and made a sweeping motion with her right arm. The furnishings were feminine, the meaning crystal clear.

When she showed me the study and the glass case where Jack kept his pearl-handled gun and the ribbons he'd won for shooting, I saw the pair of men's pajamas draped over the back of the hide-a-bed.

I followed Nicole into a kitchen that had a beamed ceiling and skylight. She fixed herself a Johnny Walker and water and got me another can of beer. I drank half of it in two swallows.

"Did you have a pool in your yard?" I asked, looking out a window at what appeared in the darkness to be a heart-shaped slab of concrete.

"Yes," she answered flatly. "But I wouldn't use it after my son drowned. So Jack's building a deck." She leaned against the counter about five feet away, both hands holding the cocktail glass, as if she was afraid she might drop it. There was no emotion in her expression or in her steel gray eyes.

"My son didn't drown in the pool," she said, reading my thoughts. "It was a fishing accident up north near the Canadian border." Her eyes looked up as if remembering. "He and Jack were camping. And when they weren't camping, they were hunting and fishing." Looking at me again, she said, "Jack's a real man, you know."

Embarrassed by the sarcastic tone of her voice, I felt my cheeks flush. I drank more beer.

"A storm came up. There were warnings, but Jack didn't pay much attention. He always knows best." Her laugh sounded like a dry cough. She drained the Scotch in one long swallow. My eyes focused on the red lip print on the edge of her glass. "Jack Junior was a good swimmer for a ten-year-old," she continued. "He spent hours in the pool. But the water up north was cold and choppy. Searchers looked for days. They never found his body." Her knuckles were white. I kept waiting for the glass to break in her hands.

"I'm sorry."

She gazed silently at me for a time before she said, "I don't know why I told you that. I guess I've needed to talk with someone. I've needed to talk with someone for a long time."

I nodded my head, unsure what, if anything, I should say.

"You're a nice guy," she said, her eyes still holding mine.

I became aware of the heat between my legs and averted my eyes. *If I were such a nice guy*, I thought, *I wouldn't have these feelings*. "I'd better go now."

"Do you want to go, Michael?"

I forced myself to look at her again, at the full lips that were slightly parted, at the smooth skin, at her breasts and nipples that pushed hard against her knit sweater. I wasn't even in her league. Maybe that was part of my excitement. I'd never been with anyone like her.

"No," I said. "Not yet."

She set her cocktail glass carefully on the counter top, straightened, and came toward me, hands at her sides. She stopped directly in front of me, her mouth close to mine.

I swallowed hard, holding my beer can between us like a shield.

"Please," she said softly.

I tried shaking my head. It didn't move.

"Please," she said again.

A voice inside my head cried "No," but the urge was too strong. I took her in my arms.

* * *

It's ten-thirty, according to the dashboard clock in my car, when I recognize the sign entering Dakota Lake. I don't remember where I've driven, or how I've arrived back where I started, only that it's been about an hour since I left Jack Stone's party.

I get off the freeway and drive into town, past Scarpelli's Italian Restaurant and the SuperAmerica station. As I brake, the Chevy slows gradually to thirty. The choke is set too high, and the car runs at least ten miles an hour without my ever having to touch the gas pedal. I need to get the choke adjusted before winter. Then I tell myself that at 120,000 miles, the Chevy will be lucky to see another winter.

I make a turn and head north toward my apartment. The air smells of diesel exhaust and is thick with the electricity of an approaching storm. Leaves and grasses tremble in anticipation.

When I come to Shore Drive, I turn left, following the winding road. Wind gusts shake the tree branches. Thunder rumbles as lightning knifes across the sky, cutting open the clouds. Rain falls. Not hard, but the drops are thick and heavy, and they make a slapping sound as they hit the tar pavement. I close the windows and turn on the wipers. The drops come harder. I concentrate on the road ahead, on the white center line, straining to see, using my sleeve to wipe condensation off the windshield because the defroster barely works.

I find no open parking spots along the curb in front of my apartment building, so I drive down a block and park in a NO PARKING zone around the corner. The neighborhood is quiet. Streetlights shimmer in the rain. I flick off the ignition. It continues to pour, hitting like BBs on the car roof.

My eyelids are heavy. Settling against the car door, I imagine myself a little kid again, riding in the backseat of the family car, an ear pressed against the seat covers, feeling the motion, hearing the hum of the tires underneath me. Life was so much simpler then. I never had to worry about where I was going—or how to get there.

I turn up my collar and lean my head against the cool window glass. The rain has to let up soon.

Chapter 4

I've had a recurring dream for the past five years.

In it I'm wandering the pale white corridors of a hospital. Nurses and doctors, busy with their tasks, seem unaware of my presence. Down a long hallway I see a dark-haired woman, dressed in a surgical gown, walking into a room. I hurry to catch her, but by the time I get there, she's gone. It goes on like that, over and over, till I come to a room where the woman lies on a huge canopy bed. Tentacle-like tubes attached to her arms are writhing snakes as they extend upwards away from her, into a bank of dark clouds. A priest stands next to the bed, administering last rites.

As I approach, I recognize Laura's face, see the pleading look in her eyes, hear the echo of her voice calling out to me, "You promised me, Michael. You promised." And then I feel the orderlies grabbing my arms, dragging me out of the room. Struggling to free myself, I awake, as I do now, trembling in a clammy sweat.

It takes a moment for me to orient myself, to realize that I have fallen asleep in my car, that I haven't actually been in the hospital, but rather I was dreaming about Laura again. I want to forget the dream though I know I can never forget. I have sought shelter in the shadows for too long now. It's only a matter of time before I finally let her memory lead me toward the light, where the twisted wreckage of my past awaits me.

I glance at my watch. Seven-thirty. Sunday morning. I straighten up and rub the stiffness out of my neck. Low clouds diffuse the rays of sunlight that manage to break through, and a foggy mist rises like wisps of gauze from the ground. Shivering,

I start the car and drive around the block till I find a parking spot closer to my apartment.

My tennis shoes squeak as I walk across the damp grass to the sidewalk and the square, two-story brick building that stands on the corner of a residential neighborhood. I can see the front window of my second-floor apartment, where I have a clear view of the trailer court on the other side of the street. The back window looks out on the alley and the garage I can't afford to rent.

My apartment has a kitchen, a bathroom, and a living room. A foldout couch doubles as a bed. I own an oak veneer dresser, a nightstand and small bookshelf, none of which match, and an overstuffed chair with loose springs. The worn green carpet in the living room is roughly the same color as the walls. The rent is low and the mice population high. Occasionally the landlord, a tobacco-chewing, retired fellow named Quint Carlson, lends me his calico cat, Buster. In the eleven months I've been here, Buster has gained a considerable amount of weight.

Once inside I take a long, hot shower, bending and stretching, loosening the knots in my shoulders and lower back. Then I towel off, drink a glass of orange juice, set the alarm for noon, and lie down to try and get more sleep.

* * *

Four hours later I drive to my parents' house. It matters little that I'd rather spend the day in bed. My mother has invited me for Sunday dinner. Though I've had legitimate excuses the last few times she's asked me over, she still has a way of making me feel guilty about turning down an invitation.

I park behind my brother's van. I look forward to the dinner but not the noise level. Rick and his wife, Joan, have three children, Jason, age twelve, Timmy, age six, and Amy, age four. You would have thought they had twenty.

My parents own a three-bedroom, single-family home in an area of nearly identical-looking houses. They're the last of a generation whose children have grown up and moved away. A second generation of homeowners lives in the neighborhood now. Strollers and baby carriages roll along the sidewalks under a spreading canopy of oaks and maples that were planted to replace the elms that succumbed to disease. Once again the yards are alive with the shouts of young children and mothers calling them home for dinner. Though the newer homes were built over the field where we first played, Oak Grove has remained much the same through the years. I feel that sense of timelessness, that permanence that touches me now. Part of me lives forever in this neighborhood—perhaps the very best part.

Dinner is scheduled for 1:00 p.m. I open the back door at 1:15. My mother stands over the stove. Her dark hair is threaded with gray, though her complexion is smooth and soft. The aroma of pot roast fills the air. She stops stirring gravy and gives me a look over her shoulder that says there's no sense in coming if you're going to just eat and run.

I come up behind her, slip my arms around her narrow waist, and kiss her on the cheek. "Sorry I'm late."

"I was beginning to think you weren't coming," she says in a tone that suggests my tardiness isn't completely forgiven.

"Where's everyone?"

As if in reply, a child yelps from the living room and then bursts into sobs. I hear my sister-in-law say, "Timmy. Give it to your sister. Right now."

"But it's mine," Timmy hollers.

"Let her have it. Please."

The television in the background is tuned to the Twins game.

"There's beer in the refrigerator," Mother says. "We'll eat as soon as I mash the potatoes."

"Good. I'm hungry."

"Where's Pam?" she asks. "I thought you were going to invite her."

I've forgotten to ask her. "She had to go home this weekend to see her parents," I lie as an excuse.

"That's too bad. Is something the matter?"

"Of course not," I say defensively. "Pam and I are getting along fine."

"I meant with her folks."

"Oh." I laugh nervously. "No. They're fine."

For a moment, my mother stares at the glass casserole cover on the counter as if it's a crystal ball. Then she looks at me.

I can't meet those blue eyes, those eyes that still cry at the sappiest Mother's Day card, the corniest television show, eyes that, like a serum, can draw the truth out of me.

"You're still dating Pam, aren't you?"

"Yes," I say, concentrating on the apple pie on the kitchen table. "Why wouldn't I be?"

"Well," she replies, waving a long wooden tablespoon at me, "I know how you are."

Joan comes into the kitchen, interrupting the discussion. I'm relieved.

"Michael," she says, giving me a hug. "How've you been?"

"Fine." Twelve years and three children ago, Joan was thin. Now, hugging her is like squeezing a down pillow.

"You're looking good."

"You, too, Joan." *What's one more lie*?

"Do you need any help, Rose?" Joan says.

"Thanks, but everything will be ready soon."

The kitchen is my mother's workshop, her private domain. She still calls herself a housewife, unconcerned that the word has almost become an obscenity.

I take a cold beer out of the refrigerator and go into the living room. My nephew, Timmy, comes running over to me, shouting, "Michael! Michael!" He throws his arms around my left leg while I ruffle his brown hair.

Joan, believing that Timmy, a rather precocious child, might be another Einstein, had him tested by a school psychologist. When the results showed Timmy to be average, Joan called the psychologist "crazy."

"Can we go outside and play catch after dinner, Michael?" Timmy asks. "I brought my glove."

"Maybe."

"Come on, Michael," he pleads. "Dad said you used to play baseball all the time. He said you were a great pitcher."

I look at my brother, Rick, sitting on the couch. He takes a long pull on a can of beer.

"And now you won't play at all anymore," Timmy continues. "Why, Michael? Why won't you play anymore?"

"I'll see how I feel later," I reply, keeping my eyes on my brother.

"Great," Timmy says, skipping into the kitchen. "We can eat now, Grandma. Michael's here."

"Rick," I say.

Rick nods. Amy, sitting next to her father on the couch, holding a plastic replica of an Uzi, smiles when I say, "Hi." Then she giggles and buries her face in her dad's denim shirt.

"Where's Jason?" I ask.

"He's spending the weekend with Joan's parents," Rick replies. "We're picking him up after we leave here." Rick's expression is one of constant weariness, as if he is functioning without sleep.

"Dad," I say, shaking his thick, calloused hand.

Dressed in his usual khaki shirt and pants, his blond hair thinning on top, my father leans back in a recliner and says, "Sit down."

Everything—the solid walnut dining room table, the leather hassock, the console television, and the hutch filled with dishes passed down from grandparents—looks the same.

My gaze lingers on my brother and his sagging jowls and potbelly. Standing in front of the bathroom mirror this morning, I noticed the slight paunch in my own midsection; how far I had to suck in my stomach to give it that flat appearance. I need to start working out again, get myself into shape. *Tomorrow,* I think. *Tomorrow I'll do a hundred sit-ups. Well, maybe just fifty.*

I sit down in an overstuffed chair. The Twins are playing the Mets in an interleague game in New York. Now the memories of the green grass, soft and cool beneath my spikes, the steady drone of the crowd, the voices of the vendors hawking their wares, the smell of hot dogs and mustard, come drifting back to me like a lazy fly ball on a sunny afternoon.

"How's business?" I say to my father. He owns a small trucking company that hauls freight throughout the Midwest. Rick manages the company.

"We've always got plenty of work to do," he answers.

I almost say, "And you think I don't?" but my mother calls out that dinner is ready, and I don't want to start anything with my father.

When we're all seated around the dining room table, my father performs the Sunday ritual, cutting the pot roast with a large butcher knife, refusing to use the electric carving knife Rick and Joan gave him.

Then my mother says, "Who's going to say grace?"

No one volunteers. After everyone takes turns nominating everyone else, a consensus is finally reached, and Timmy is chosen. This delights Joan, and she offers that her children have been attending church regularly.

I'm reminded of the time in college when, with two strikes and the bases loaded, I pleaded with God to let me get a hit. I struck out. My relationship with Him hasn't been the same since.

As we all fold our hands and bow our heads, Timmy blurts, "Thanks for the food, thanks for the meat, yea God, let's eat." He looks around the table, apparently waiting for applause.

"Timothy!" Joan says, appalled. "Where in the world did you learn that?"

Timmy now looks as if he doesn't understand what he's done wrong.

"Tim-o-thy," Joan says again, but this time with just the hint of a threat.

"In Sunday school," he replies.

"You did not."

Timmy, bottom lip quivering, says, "I did so."

"Don't talk back to me, young man."

Tears well up in Timmy's eyes.

"I want some milk," Amy whines.

"Hush," Joan says.

My mother, as always, coming to the defense of the persecuted, says to Timmy, "It's okay, honey." He bursts into tears.

Joan looks at Rick and says, "Can you believe Timmy learned that in Sunday school?"

Rick just shrugs.

Later, after Timmy quiets down and Amy gets her milk, my father looks at me and says, "So, do you have a teaching job for next year?"

When I fail to respond, he continues.

"They let you go again, huh? All that education and—"

"No, they didn't let me go. As a matter of fact, they offered me a contract for next year." I have no time to think about what I'm saying. At that moment I just want my father to believe that becoming a teacher has been the right choice and that finally something good has come of it.

"That's wonderful, Michael," my mother says, folding her hands as if to thank the Lord.

I regret having lied, but only because of her.

"Hey," Rick says, perking up, raising his glass of milk in a toast.

"Congratulations," Joan adds.

"It's about time," my father says as he resumes eating his dinner.

* * *

That night in my apartment, I sit on the foldout couch, staring at the dresser where my baseball trophies once were lined up, recalling my father's response when I told him I had a teaching job for next year. Even though I know why he was upset, I still have trouble accepting it. I remember when I was younger I thought that Rick had a better understanding of our father's disposition. It wasn't until a few hours before Rick was to be married that I learned I wasn't the only one who had felt the pressure to please. My older brother had felt it, too, perhaps even more than me.

* * *

We were alone together in Rick's room about an hour before leaving the house for the church. I was sixteen. It was two years before my high school team would go undefeated and win the state baseball championship, two years before I would get a scholarship to pitch for the University of Minnesota.

I was watching Rick as he stood in front of his dresser mirror, adjusting his bow tie and cummerbund. All around the room were pennants and pictures of great baseball players like Hank Aaron and Johnny Bench.

"You still working on an off-speed pitch?" he asked.

"You know I am. I can hear Dad's voice in my sleep. 'If you want to be a great pitcher, you've got to learn to throw an off-speed pitch.'"

Rick laughed. "Remember the game for the legion championship last summer? A lot of the Major League scouts were there to see Jake Walker pitch. It was the last game I ever caught for you."

"How could I forget?"

"Dad figured it was a golden opportunity for you to show them you were as good or better than Walker."

"I was better than Walker."

"Now you are," Rick said, turning around and leaning against the dresser. "I don't know about then."

"Hey, we were ahead one-zip in the bottom of the seventh."

Rick nodded as he remembered. "They had the top of the order coming up, but you got two quick outs before you walked their number three batter, Clark, on four pitches. Coach Olive and I came out to the mound and asked if you were tired."

"And I told him I'd struck Walker out twice, and I could get him again."

"Yeah. And sure enough, you blew two fastballs right by him."

"I should've thrown him a change on the next pitch," I said, thinking back on it, seeing it clearly in my mind, getting upset all over again, as if it were yesterday. "Why did you call for another fastball, Rick? I wanted to throw the change."

"Dad wanted you to throw a change, too," Rick said.

"How do you know that?"

"While you were rubbing up the ball, I looked up in the stands and made eye contact with Dad. He was looking down at me, and I could read his lips. "Change up."

"And you still called for a fastball?"

"Yeah."

"Why? You knew Dad was right. I could've gotten Walker. We would've won the game."

"Maybe," Rick said. "But Walker beat you that day, buddy, not me. If you had thrown that fastball in on his fists where I wanted it, Walker would've never hit it out of the park and won the game."

"I was tired, Rick. You knew that."

He nodded.

"Then why?"

"I don't know," he said with a shrug. "I think it had more to do with Dad than you."

"Dad?"

"Yeah," he said, turning sideways to look at himself in profile.

"I don't get it."

"I wouldn't worry about it now, buddy. It's over."

"Then why tell me about it in the first place? I can't believe you went against Dad's advice."

"Sometimes I can't believe it myself."

"You know, Rick, you could've gone to college. Maybe even played pro ball."

"That's what you want, Mike. Not me."

"What is it you want?"

"Joan," he said with a wink and a smile.

"Besides Joan."

"Why the sudden curiosity?"

"Because in two hours you'll be married and living in some other house, and I don't think we'll ever get a chance to talk like this again."

Rick picked up his white dinner jacket and was about to put it on when he hesitated. "Hey, buddy, it's not like I'm leaving the state."

"I know that. But I thought you wanted to play pro ball."

"Ah, playing baseball for a living was only a pipe dream."

"But it was your dream."

"And that's all it ever was. A dream." He put on his jacket and took one last look at himself in the mirror. "I guess what I want to do now is take over Dad's business someday."

"There's more to it than that," I said, looking away.

"What's that supposed to mean?"

I kept my eyes on the poster of Johnny Bench on the wall.

"Come on," Rick urged.

"Joan's pregnant, isn't she?"

"Where'd you get that idea?"

"I heard Mom and Dad talking about it."

Rick sat down on the bed next to me. "It isn't what you think."

"You gave up baseball and college because of Joan," I said, staring hard at him, surprised at the disappointment and anger I suddenly felt.

"No," he replied, shaking his head. "It isn't Joan's fault."

"But if she hadn't gotten pregnant, then—"

"Wait a minute, buddy." He stood. "You've got it wrong. All wrong." He walked over to a window and stood with his back to me. Finally he said, "It was my idea. Not hers."

"What?"

He turned around to face me. "I convinced Joan to go off the pill," he said. "I wanted her to get pregnant."

"But why, Rick? Why would you want to do that?"

He stared at me for a long time before he said, "I just wanted out of baseball, and I needed an excuse. An excuse Dad could live with."

* * *

My cell phone on the nightstand next to my bed rings, pulling me back to the present. My stomach is still full from the pot roast at my parents' house, and I feel heavy and slow as I roll over on my bed. The phone rings again, and I wonder if it's Pam. It rings once more. *I can't avoid her forever.* I reach over and pick up the phone. "Hello?"

"Mike?"

My heartbeat slows considerably. "Hi, Mac."

"You hear yet?" he asks.

"Hear what?"

He hesitates.

"What, Mac?"

"Kate Fleming died this evening."

Chapter 5

Monday is as black as any Monday I remember. Flashes of lightning branch across the charcoal sky, illuminating trees and telephone poles, distorting their shapes in such a way that I think I'm looking at a surrealistic painting. Thunder rumbles like the engine on Mac's Harley, and the old school building reverberates with it.

It's the last week of classes before summer vacation. Graduation ceremonies are scheduled for Friday night. Amid the storm and the sorrow over Kate Fleming's death, students try to study for their final exams, which begin the next day. Kate has taught and coached at Wilson High for twenty years. Her former students number in the thousands. She succeeded with troubled kids because she walked that fine line between permissiveness and discipline using "tough love." Even those students at Wilson who didn't know her sense the loss, and tears punctuate the day.

As I head for the lounge during my lunch period, Bob Haber, the assistant principal, passes me in the hallway, doing his daily race walk around the building. He wears a powder blue, nylon warm-up suit and matching Reeboks. Arms pumping, concentration etched on his brow, he doesn't see me.

The storm outside has abated, but a steady rain falls, and drops drum against the windowpanes. I find two notes in my mailbox in the lounge. One is a message to call Pam. The other is from Jack Stone asking me to see him ASAP. An alarm clangs inside my head. *God, he knows!*

I decide to call Pam first.

Her secretary answers and says, "One moment."

It turns out to be more than a moment.

"Hello, Michael," she says, with no inflection in her voice.

"I'm sorry I didn't call you earlier."

Silence.

I wait, wondering how or even if I should proceed. "I'd like to get together and talk," I say at last. "Straighten everything out."

"I don't know that there's anything to talk about."

I have an urge to say, "Then why did you call?" and end the conversation right there. "Look, Pam, I know I've been a jerk."

"Jerk is much too kind a word." It's the first time I have known her to be angry. It surprises me, though it's certainly understandable.

"I just want to explain what happened at the restaurant on Friday."

There's a pause.

After a time she says, "I don't know, Michael." Some of the anger in her voice has been replaced by hurt.

"Please. Just give me a chance to explain."

"When?" she asks hesitantly.

"Tonight. Tomorrow night. Whenever you want."

Another pause.

"All right," she says. "Tuesday night at my place. About seven."

"Would you like to have dinner?"

"No," she replies and hangs up.

I stop in the faculty men's room and splash cold water on my face. As I towel off, I look at myself in the mirror and see my wan complexion and the dark stubble on my cheeks and chin. Did I forget to shave this morning? How could I? I had everything timed to the minute. No wasted motion, just a quick shower, the shave, a piece of toast and a glass of orange juice. Ten minutes to school.

Turning away from the mirror, I slip on a puddle of water. It reminds me of the time last winter when I was driving along in a daze and suddenly hit a patch of glare ice. My life, it seems, is spinning out of control. *I have to maintain control. Get myself headed in the right direction. Any direction.* I take some time to compose myself. Then I head for the main office.

Jack Stone's secretary, Elaine Samuels, is on the phone talking in that husky voice of hers, which sounds as if it belongs to a linebacker. She acknowledges my presence with a smile and a nod, and cups a hand over the receiver. "I've got a great joke to tell you, Michael," she whispers.

"Is it dirty?"

"Of course," she says with a hearty laugh.

Behind and to the right of Elaine's desk, Beth Stanton comes out of Jack Stone's office. Both she and Jack are smiling. Jack leans closer to her, says something, and they both start laughing.

Shit. He's hired Beth for Kate's position.

Beth shakes Jack's hand and turns to leave. Noticing me, she smiles. "Hello, Michael."

"Hello."

"I'm collecting money for Kate's flowers," she says.

"I don't have any cash on me."

"That's okay. I'll catch you later."

"Ready, Collins?" Jack Stone's voice booms.

For what?

I follow Jack into his office and sit down in a cushioned chair, imagining for an instant that I'm an innocent man sitting in the electric chair. Then again, I can hardly think of myself as innocent. Jack closes the door behind him.

On the walls hang pictures of Jack in his flight suit standing next to his fighter plane and crew; Jack standing next to his pickup with a big buck strapped in the back; Jack standing next to a huge marlin he caught off the Florida Keys. On his desk is a framed picture of a much younger Nicole and their late son, Jack Jr. Nicole is resting on one knee, smiling broadly, an arm draped around the shoulder of her small son. But it's the utter joy in Nicole's eyes that holds my gaze. It's a look she has not shown me, a look that perhaps neither Jack nor I will ever see again.

"Collins . . ." Jack says, hitching up his trousers and sitting down in the swivel chair behind his desk. The chair squeals, pleading for mercy.

I never liked Jack calling me "Collins," but I figure now is a poor time to protest.

"I hate to talk business so soon after a tragedy."

I nod.

"I knew Kate for nearly twenty years. In fact, we started in the district together. She was a damn fine person. The kind you don't find much anymore. She's going to be missed."

For a moment I believe I detect tears in Jack's eyes.

Then he says, "But as much as I liked and respected her, decisions have to be made."

I keep nodding and staring at the top of Jack's smooth head, which shines as if it's been waxed.

Jack clasps the fingers of his large hands on his desk and rolls his shoulders like he's loosening up for a fight. I remember seeing him in the shower once after a student versus faculty basketball game. His body, large and powerful, was as hairy as an ape's.

"We're fortunate here at Wilson," he says, "because we have very capable people to replace those who have . . ." he pauses, as if searching for the right word, ". . . left us."

I look at Jack's biceps bulging out of his short-sleeved shirt. *What would he do to me if he found out I was sleeping with Nicole?*

"Now, you and I have had our differences throughout the year, Collins."

That's putting it mildly. Whether it's requesting more money for textbooks and materials, or persuading reluctant staff members to adapt their curriculum for special education students, Jack has been slow on the draw.

"But differences aside, quite frankly, Collins, I think you're a damn fine teacher."

I look into Jack Stone's eyes, which are deep-set and as brown as the cigars he likes to smoke. "What?" I say, uncertain if I've heard him correctly.

"I said that I think you're a fine teacher. Of course, we have to go through the normal bullshit of posting the position and interviewing the candidates. But I'm quite confident that after all is said and done, you'll have yourself a job for next year."

It suddenly strikes me that I haven't lied to my father about finding a full-time job for next year after all.

Jack stands up and extends a hand. "Welcome aboard."

"You're offering me Kate's position?" I say as I rise and reach across the desktop to shake Jack's hand.

He grins. "You don't want it?"

"Of course I do. Why wouldn't I?"

I haven't quite sorted out my feelings as Jack escorts me out of the office. He pats me on the back and leaves me standing in the hallway amid a crush of students hurrying to lunch.

"Hey! Mr. C!"

I turn in the direction of the voice as one of my students, Danny O'Brien, approaches. Danny is a wiry kid about five feet ten, with red hair and eyes that are as blue as the mood of the school.

"I got a real problem, Mr. C. Bruder told me I need to get a B on my English final in order to pass the course."

"I thought you were doing fine in English."

"No. It was Econ I was doing fine in. Remember?"

"Right. Econ. Well, we'll review tomorrow. You'll pass."

"But Bruder told me he won't let you read the final test to me."

"When did he tell you that?"

"In class a few minutes ago. You've got to talk to him again, Mr. C. If I fail English, my father will . . ." He stops.

"He'll what, Danny?"

Danny shakes his head. "Nothing."

"You're worried about what he might say?"

"You don't know my father."

"And you don't know mine," I reply without thinking.

He stares at me a moment. "What does that mean?"

"It means that I understand. And I will talk to Bruder."

"Promise?"

The word jolts me.

"You okay, Mr. C? You got real pale all of a sudden."

My reaction must have shown on my face. "I'm fine. Just stay calm, Danny, and get to your next class on time. Don't worry about Bruder. I'll straighten everything out."

Chapter 6

Back in my apartment at the end of the day, I sit on the couch drinking a cold beer, looking out a window at dark, puffy clouds that loom like artillery fire on the horizon. I decide that I should call someone, that I should tell someone the good news; I've finally been offered a continuing teaching contract, though it never would have happened had Kate Fleming not died. I pick up the phone to call Pam but quickly dismiss the idea.

I finish two more beers as I continue watching the clouds march across the sky till the first pearl-shaped drop of rain explodes against the pane. It occurs to me at that moment that I have no one to share my good news with, that I haven't shared much of anything since Laura.

* * *

"Pardon me." She stood in the aisle of the 757, an arm resting on the back of my seat, holding a thick paperback book in one hand. "Do you mind if I sit next to you? I'm having a problem getting my headphones to work. I thought I'd try another seat."

She was medium height and had olive skin. Her thick hair was dark and shoulder-length, so different from the more familiar blond, fair-skinned women of the Midwest. But it was her eyes that I focused on, green eyes that were animated and full of spirit.

"Mind? No. Of course not."

"Thank you." She slid into the empty seat next to me. "My name's Laura. Laura Aubrey." She offered a hand.

It felt as soft and delicate as silk. "Michael Collins."

"Are you going to St. Thomas?"

"San Juan."

"Vacation?"

I shook my head. "I'm a pitcher in the Mets' organization. I'm on my way to San Juan to play winter ball. I have to report in four days."

"So you're playing baseball year round?"

"Not all of us do. But I'm working on a pitch. A change-up." I started to explain, but she cut me off.

"I know what a change-up is. I could out-hit and out-throw most of the boys in my neighborhood."

"You're certainly not a ballplayer."

"No," she said with a smile. "I teach English at the University of Minnesota. Actually, I'm only a teaching assistant. I'm working on my doctorate."

"My degree's in education, too."

"Really? What subject?"

"Physical education," I said with a shrug.

Her smile put me at ease. "Seems we have something in common." She put on her headphones and adjusted the volume control located on the arm of the seat. Then she opened the book in her hand and began reading.

I settled back in my seat and tried to think of something witty to say to her. Thirty minutes later I was still thinking. I wanted to look at her, to look into those beautiful eyes again, but I didn't want to appear obvious. So I stole sidelong glances, feeling uncomfortable and frustrated.

When a flight attendant came by, I ordered a beer.

"That sounds good," Laura said, removing the headphones. "I'll have the same."

I took the opportunity to ask her what she was reading.

She handed me the book. "It's an Emily Dickinson poem, number 341. I'm writing my dissertation on Dickinson."

After great pain, a formal feeling comes—
The Nerves sit ceremonious, like Tombs—
The stiff Heart questions 'was it He that bore,'
And 'Yesterday, or Centuries before'?

The Feet, mechanical, go round—
A Wooden way
Of Ground, or Air or Ought—
Regardless grown,
A Quartz contentment, like a stone—

This is the Hour of Lead
Remembered, if outlived,
As Freezing persons, recollect the Snow—
First – Chill—then Stupor—then the letting go—

I was uncertain of the poem's meaning and embarrassed to ask, though the line, *a quartz contentment like a stone,* kept running through my head like a vinyl record stuck in a groove.

"Dickinson lived a very secluded life. In fact, she didn't leave her house for over fifteen years. Neighbors called her the Myth."

I wanted to shift the subject from poetry and Emily Dickinson. I passed her the book. "I'm afraid I don't read much poetry."

"Not all of Dickinson's poetry is so somber. She really did write some beautiful love poems."

Suddenly, I was interested in poetry again. "Really?"

Laura nodded as the flight attendant returned with our drinks. "To vacations," Laura said, touching her plastic cup against mine.

"To Dickinson."

She peered into my eyes and smiled, causing adrenaline to rush through me so quickly I thought I might need an oxygen mask. I took a long pull on my beer before I said, "Do you have family living in Minnesota?"

"No. My mother and father are both deceased."

"Brothers and sisters?"

"No siblings. You?"

"My parents live in Oak Grove. I have an older brother who's married."

There was a pause before she said, "I hope we haven't run out of things in common."

"Not yet. We're both single."

"How do you know?"

"Lucky guess," I said, knowing full well it was wishful thinking. "And we're both traveling alone."

"Correct. And I've noticed you're left-handed."

"You, too?"

"Yes."

"See, we have lots in common."

When the plane hit a little pothole of turbulence, I glanced out the window at the blue beauty of the sky and the ocean far below, the still water appearing so close I felt as though I could reach out and touch it. I listened to the hum of the jet engines and the beating of my heart, and I wished I had more time before I had to report to my team.

"Where are you staying in St. Thomas?" I asked, looking at her again.

"At Frenchman's Reef."

"I've never been to St. Thomas. Have you?"

She nodded and rested her gaze on me. "It's warm and wonderful," she said and proceeded to tell me all about the island.

Later, I told her about my baseball career. We were still talking when the downward whine of the flaps and the popping of my ears signaled our descent into San Juan. I heard the landing gear lower and the seat belt sign chime, and soon a flight attendant began her customary landing and departure speech.

When Laura and I said our goodbyes in San Juan, I felt a sudden emptiness. The feeling remained throughout the evening. I was alone in a strange city and would be for a few more days, but I knew the emptiness I felt was not born out of loneliness.

Unable to sleep much, I rose early the next morning. I was disgusted with myself for not asking Laura if she'd like to spend some time together and nervous about calling her.

I finished unpacking my suitcase and then, as I began emptying my carry-on bag, I discovered Laura's copy of Dickinson. Inside the cover of the book she'd written:

You may have misjudged her. Why not give her another chance?

I looked at the note once more. I was no poet or an English major, but I didn't have to be to read between the lines. I found a Dickinson poem that I liked and sent it off to her in two text messages:

Laura,

Wild nights! Wild nights!
Were I with thee,
Wild nights should be
Our luxury!
Futile the winds
To a heart in port,
Done with the compass,
Done with the chart.

Rowing in Eden!
Ah! the sea!
Might I but moor
Tonight in thee!

Then I went for a run along the beach. When I returned to my room, my cell phone beeped with a text message.

Michael. You have excellent taste in poetry. I'd like to hear more. Laura.

I packed a bag and caught a cab to the airport.

* * *

I took Laura shopping along the narrow streets and outdoor cafes of French town and to the Atlantic side of the island, where we sunbathed on the white sand beaches of Magen's Bay.

Before lunch we rented mopeds and toured the island, which was hilly and green with lots of flowers and stucco buildings with red tile roofs. Though she'd never been on a scooter before, Laura learned quickly. Soon she was running full out, enjoying the freedom and the speed as we raced up and down the hills and around the curves and narrow roads, never faltering or backing off the throttle.

In the afternoon we boarded a ferry for the twenty-minute boat ride from Red Hook across Pillsbury Sound to Trunk Bay on the island of St. John, with its lush forest of bay trees. The waters of the Caribbean were clear and warm. We snorkeled together, following the underwater trails with their red and blue flora and coral formations, and fed the thousands of multi-colored fish that swarmed like bees around us. Laura was a dolphin in the water, completely fearless. We swam way out past the markers, laughing, diving and splashing about. I felt like a kid in high school again, experiencing my first crush.

Lying beside her on the sugar-white beach, I covered myself with sun block and marveled at how quickly she tanned. I caught myself continually looking at her, at the tilt of her head as she paused to consider something, at her dark hair and delicate hands; the way she used her thumb and forefinger to pull a bill out of her wallet, as if she was picking a piece of lint off a sweater.

That night we dined in a quiet restaurant without walls, under a thatched roof beside the ocean. A full moon painted a thin coat of white across the surface of the water; waves brushed gently against the shoreline, the sound of jazz-fusion from somewhere drifting in on the breeze. Laura's simple, white cotton dress was bright against her olive skin. Her dark hair was plaited, and her eyes shone turquoise in the soft light.

"Did you come here for the weather?" I asked.

"No." Candlelight reflected off the wine glass in her hand. "I came here to forget someone."

Have you forgotten him yet? I wanted to say, but I knew it was too soon.

After dinner we drank *piña coladas* in the bar and walked along the beach under millions of stars blown like sparks about the sky. We carried our shoes, held hands, and listened to the soothing rhythm of the waves. We spoke little, but there was little that needed to be said. Above us, the moon looked worn, as if it had once been a shell washed by time's waters.

Later, when I stood holding her tightly in the entryway of her hotel room, getting as close as our clothes would allow, kissing her and feeling it as though for the first time, I knew that I was falling in love with Laura, that I had imagined loving someone like her all of my life.

"Make love to me, Michael," she whispered.

I did.

* * *

That winter we kept up a constant correspondence between Santurce, Puerto Rico, and St. Paul, Minnesota, e-mailing three and four times a week, and when e-mails didn't satisfy my hunger for communication, I called Laura, accumulating a stiff phone bill that ate up much of my meager salary.

When I returned home to St. Paul in February, two days before I had to report for spring training in Port St. Lucie, Florida, I stayed with her. She lived in a rented side-by-side duplex off Como Avenue near the state fairgrounds and St. Anthony, not far from the University of Minnesota.

The duplex was an older two-story structure with a screened porch in front. The interior itself was sparsely furnished. I assumed it was because Laura was a teaching assistant without much money, but later I realized that she placed little value on "things" and on money in general.

In the living room was a wicker couch with floral print cushions stitched in red and blue patterns, a large oriental rug covering the hardwood floor, and an upright piano that had belonged to her mother, who she said had died of cancer a few years ago. A rectangular mirror and walnut cabinets with a serving area were built into one wall of the dining room, facing a walnut table and four chairs.

Upstairs in her bedroom were some bookshelves she'd made out of bricks and pine boards. The shelves were filled with hardcovers and paperbacks, poetry by Whitman and Byron and Shelley, novels by Joyce and Lawrence and Woolf. There were no photos of friends or family.

Laura raised a glass of wine and said,

"Wine comes in at the mouth
And love comes in at the eye;
That's all we shall know for truth
Before we grow old and die.
I lift the glass to my mouth,
I look at you, and I sigh."

There was something in her smile, something in her face and eyes that remained a child.

"Did you write that poem?"

She shook her head. "Yeats wrote it."

"To us," I said as our glasses clinked together.

* * *

We were sitting at her dining room table the night before I had to leave for spring training, enjoying the last of a bottle of red wine. Her dark hair was pulled back in a ponytail. Bangs swept across her forehead, and I thought she looked more like a student than a college teacher.

"Are you happy, Michael?"

"Yes. I'm in love."

I'd always been reluctant to express those feelings. I suppose it was because I feared I'd be rejected, though there were times when I knew I wouldn't be. But in retrospect, I really hadn't loved anyone in the same way that I loved Laura. Now the words "I love you" rolled off my lips as easily as a kiss.

"What is it you love about me?"

"Your cute ass."

"I'm serious."

"So am I."

"Come on," she coaxed, looking into my eyes, searching, I imagined, for the answer to her question.

A yearning to touch her rushed through me at that moment, and I covered her hand with mine and tried to think of a profound, mysterious reason that made our love unique, that made me love her the way I did. Certainly I loved the way she looked; I couldn't deny that, but there had to be something more.

"You're open and trusting," I said, trying to find the words to describe a feeling that was, for me, indescribable. "Though I worry sometimes that people take advantage of you."

"You're the only one I let take advantage of me."

I remembered reading that the brain produced a natural aphrodisiac when lovers were infatuated with one another, a condition called limerence. Maybe my feelings for Laura had more to do with body chemistry, with a rush of hormones and endorphins, but that sounded too passionless and scientific. Maybe we were lovers in a previous lifetime that recognized one another and fell in love once more. That sounded more romantic. Then again, maybe why I loved her didn't matter much at all. Maybe what really mattered was how I loved her, how I felt when I was with her, how I felt when I was without her.

"All I know is that there are only two times when I feel truly alive," I said, finally. "One is when I'm pitching. The other is when I'm with you."

She smiled again and lifted her hand and touched my cheek gently with her fingers, and I felt the sweetness of desire rise like a swift tide inside me.

"We have star equilibrium, Michael. It's a phrase from D.H. Lawrence's *Women in Love.* Lawrence says that ideal lovers should be like two stars orbiting the same hemisphere, holding each other in a magnetic field so that neither sways the other from its course. I think we have star equilibrium."

Our conversations often moved randomly from subject to subject, for Laura spoke of things as they came into her mind. It was that freshness, that spontaneity that gave our talks a certain edge and which was part of her charm. Being with her forced me to see things and talk about things I wouldn't normally talk about.

"You're smart," I said. "I like that. Most of the time."

"Not smart," she replied, tapping a fork against her wine glass, keeping up a steady rhythm. "Educated."

"I'm around a lot of ballplayers with college degrees. Most of them may be educated, but they aren't very smart."

"I think you're smart, Michael. I think you should teach."

"There aren't many physical education jobs available."

"Then why not teach in another area? An area like special education, where you can really help children."

"I don't think I'd be very good with those kinds of kids."

"How do you know till you try? Besides, you need something to fall back on when your baseball career is over."

"It's just beginning."

"Careers like yours don't last very long. You really have no time to waste."

She continued tapping her fork against her wine glass, only now her whole body was moving to the beat of some primordial rhythm.

At the time I didn't recognize the storm warnings of Laura's illness, didn't realize what was about to happen. As we grew closer, I was able to sense the subtle changes in the weather of her personality, hear the dark rumblings much earlier.

I said, "That's sort of the way you view life, isn't it?"

"What do you mean?"

"You always seem to be in such a hurry, yet you have this inexhaustible supply of energy."

She let out a sudden burst of laughter, which came more as a spasm of reaction than from enjoyment. Then she stood and began dancing around the table, laughing, giggling, mussing up my hair. There was something strange in her laughter, like unhinged delight.

"What's so funny?" I said.

"Everything," she replied. "Everything's funny. Don't you think so?" She sat down at the piano in the living room and started singing and playing, first a part of one tune, then another, like some malfunctioning player piano.

"You've had too much wine," I said, trying to contain my own laughter.

Then she stopped.

I quit laughing as a hush settled over the room like the eerie quiet just before a tornado.

She sat perfectly still for a moment before she said, "You don't want me to finish my Ph.D., do you?" She didn't look at me, but rather at the piano keys.

"What?"

"My Ph.D. You don't want me to finish it, do you?" Her voice was just above a whisper, as if she was speaking to herself.

"Of course I do."

She stood up. The piano bench slid back and tipped over with a thud. "Don't lie to me, Michael! I hate it when you lie to me!" Her eyebrows were lowered and drawn together, and her eyes stared hard at me and were filled with rage.

I sat motionless, numb, like I'd been shot full of Novocain. "What are you talking about? I've never lied to you."

"You have too lied to me, you fucker!"

The words hit me like a punch in the stomach. Gooseflesh prickled my skin, and a tingling like current began in my limbs; a sensation I recognized as fear, not for myself, but for Laura, for us.

"You're a liar, Michael!" she screamed. "A goddamn liar!" Abruptly she turned and ran upstairs. I heard the bathroom door slam, the lock click.

I ran after her, taking two steps at a time. "Laura," I called, trying to keep the edge out of my voice. "Open the door."

When she didn't respond, I knocked. "Laura. Are you all right?"

"Go away, Michael."

"What is it?" I pleaded. "What's happened?"

"I don't want you to see me like this, Michael." Her tone was softer now, like a child hoping for forgiveness.

"I don't understand what this is all about."

"Please, Michael."

I waited for a time, hoping she'd change her mind. She must have sensed my continued presence, for again she said, "Please."

"I love you, Laura." I waited longer this time before I turned and walked down the stairs and out the front door.

Chapter 7

I played Triple-A ball that summer with the Norfolk Tides in Norfolk, Virginia, in the International League, one step away from the majors. I rented the top floor of a white clapboard house with Bobby Sutter, a second baseman from Macon, Georgia.

Bobby Sutter was a quiet, religious man, a stocky five foot ten inches, with blond hair cut short around the sides. He'd been in the Mets' organization for five years. He'd split last year between Binghamton and Norfolk and hit a solid .270. But someone in the Mets' management thought his range was limited and that he didn't make the double play pivot fast enough. I'd played with quite a few second basemen, and Bobby was as good as any. Unfortunately, I'd also seen guys who got stuck with labels like "no hustle," or "poor arm," or "bad attitude." Once you were labeled, justified or not, it was nearly impossible to shake it. Your only chance was to get with another organization and start fresh. I knew Bobby was thinking of asking for a trade or quitting if the Mets didn't give him an opportunity in New York soon. He had a wife and a young son back home, and he missed them as much as I missed Laura.

She'd sent e-mails making light of her "tantrum," as she called it, blaming her behavior on too much wine, and the fact that she was upset because we'd been away from each other for such a long time and would soon be away from each other again. Still, the curses she'd hurled at me that night were daggers that opened deep wounds, wounds which were slow to heal and left scars. It took a while before I realized how much I missed her.

I'd call her late in the evening after games from places like Louisville and Columbus. She would usually be up, full of energy and wanting to talk forever. By July we were missing each other so much I sent her a plane ticket, and she came east for a visit.

The team had just returned from an extended road trip, and we were scheduled for a six-game home stand. I was slated to pitch Friday night against Charlotte. On Wednesday afternoon, I drove the ocean blue Mazda Miata convertible I'd bought with my signing bonus over to the airport in Norfolk to pick up Laura.

A palpable wave of excitement rushed through me when I saw her, a wave that washed away the loneliness of the road and the endless bus trips and hotel rooms and late-night meals eaten in towns filled with strangers.

She came running toward me in her yellow sundress and sandals and threw her arms around my neck and kissed me.

"God, I missed you, Michael. I missed you so much."

I kissed her and hugged her and inhaled the clean scent of her hair, the sweet fragrance of her perfume. "And I missed you."

"Did you?"

"Yes."

"Did you really?"

"Yes. Yes."

She kept her arms around my neck and her face close to mine as she looked up at me and said with a smile, "Prove it."

*   *   *

Always the southern gentleman, Bobby Sutter graciously disappeared so that just Laura and I could have the top floor of the clapboard house.

In the late afternoon light, she pressed her lips on mine. Her mouth opened and she moaned softly as our tongues touched. Passion surged like a current inside me as we shed our clothes and fell upon the bed, carried away by the electricity, moving together as in a dance, close and then closer still, always one, until the rhythm of movement was beyond stopping. I heard my voice cry out as she arched her back to receive me, her hands clutching the sheets, her whole body stiffening as she trembled uncontrollably, riding the wave within her, rolling her head from side to side as though she was struggling for air, till finally she was quiet under me.

I stroked her damp hair and gently kissed her forehead till our breathing became normal. It was in moments such as these that I believed nothing could separate us; nothing could ever pull us apart.

She rode with me to the ballpark later that evening and sat in the stands while the team took batting practice, and I did my wind sprints with the other pitchers. I'd started the season as the fourth man in a four-man rotation, but after winning five of my first six starts, my manager, Johnny Desmond, was quoted in the press as saying I was the "ace of the staff." We were playing Charlotte. They were in third place, right behind us. We were two games behind Durham, whom we played this weekend.

I spent the game sitting in the bullpen with most of the other pitchers, watching the action unfold as a critic might watch a play. It was the height of the tourist season, and Harbor Park was filled. Occasionally, I caught a glimpse of Laura as she stood and cheered a nice play in the field, or when we scored a run with a clutch hit.

Steve Lasser, a twenty-three-year-old from Sacramento, California, was pitching for us. He'd started the year number one on the staff, having won sixteen games last year in double-A ball, but he'd struggled most of this season, and his record had fallen to three and five—though he'd pitched well his last couple of times out. His curve ball was his best pitch, but for some inexplicable reason, he hadn't been able to find the plate with it in most of his starts. Frustration had taken its toll on Steve, and he'd refused to talk to the press, which he felt had been overly critical of his performance. But tonight was different. Tonight Steve was masterful. He held Charlotte to two hits, none after the fourth inning, and we won four to nothing.

* * *

On Thursday morning I took Laura sightseeing up to Williamsburg. We stopped at the Busch Gardens on the way and saw the Old Country Tudor town and Busch's version of the Globe Theatre. We drank beer at one of the sidewalk cafes and walked around the German village with its antique carousel. Then we drove on till we saw the sign to Colonial Williamsburg off of I-64, where we toured the capitol, the public gaol, Raleigh Tavern, the governor's palace, and some of the colonial craft shops. Laura wanted to see more, but I had to get back in time for the game.

Since I was pitching the next day, it was my turn to chart pitches in the dugout. I kept track of the type of pitch and the number thrown as twenty-four-year-old Todd Granger, from Waco, Texas, pitched a six-hitter, and we blew out Charlotte, seven to one, gaining a game on Durham. If we swept them this weekend, we'd be tied for first place.

I was more tense than usual on Friday morning. It was a big game, but I'd pitched in big games before. That morning after breakfast Laura said, "Let's play catch."

"You're kidding."

"Come on outside, and we'll see who's kidding whom." She borrowed Bobby's glove, and we went out to the backyard.

"Toss the ball here, big boy," she said. She was wearing one of my Mets caps on her head, an oversized Minnesota Twins sweatshirt, which nearly came down to her knees, a pair of blue tights, and white jogging shoes with pink laces and pink lightning bolts on the side. Because Bobby was right-handed, Laura wore his glove backward on her left hand.

I didn't know whether to laugh or kiss her.

"Come on," she said, with hands on hips. "Throw it."

"Okay. Let's see what you've got."

She lifted up her sweatshirt and showed me her naked breasts.

"Not bad."

"What do you mean, not bad?"

"Terrific."

"That's better," she said, pulling down the sweatshirt and pounding the glove. "Now hum it in here, baby."

"I've lost my concentration."

"Come on, you wimp. Put a little mustard on it."

"Mustard?"

"Don't you understand baseball lingo when you hear it?"

"Sorry."

I was surprised at how easily she caught the ball and by her fluid motion as she flung it back to me. I threw the ball to her again, and she caught it without blinking.

"Mix in some grounders and flies, Michael."

We played catch for a half hour. In that time she caught nearly everything I threw to her with equal ease and agility.

"Seen enough?" she said finally.

"I don't believe this."

"If you want to see more," she said, strutting toward the house, "you'll have to follow me."

* * *

My pregame meal usually consisted of carbohydrates eaten two hours before going to the park. In keeping with this tradition, I fixed spaghetti for the three of us. When Bobby and Laura entered the kitchen, where I was boiling the spaghetti noodles in hot water on an old gas stove, I said, "I believe they're ready."

"How do you know?" Laura asked.

I speared a noodle out of the rapidly boiling water with a fork and flicked the noodle against the wall. "There, you see? When a noodle sticks like that, it's done."

"Just like Julia Child," Laura said, giving me a hug.

We ate and laughed and sang along with "Escape," a Rupert Holmes song on an oldies station.

After dinner, I drove over to the ballpark with Bobby; Laura would drive over later in my car.

I felt good during warm-ups, but by the time I got to the mound and faced my first batter, I realized I was too pumped up. I walked him on four pitches, unusual for me since I walked an average of only two batters a game.

Our catcher, Dickie Moore, came out to the mound and tried to calm me down. "You're overthrowin'," he said, his mask resting on top of his head, a wad of bubble gum bulging his cheek.

"No shit."

"Relax. We got a long way to go in this one." He spit as if for emphasis.

Once he was back behind the plate, he squatted, pounded his mitt, and gave me the sign for a curve ball.

I broke one off, and the batter, having squared for a bunt attempt, popped the ball up directly in front of the plate. Dickie flung off his mask, caught the ball before it hit the ground, and in one cat-quick motion, pivoted and gunned the ball to first, nailing the runner who had started for second and now couldn't get back to first in time to beat Dickie's throw.

Two outs.

Dickie gave me a thumbs-up sign and smiled. He looked somewhat deranged, which you damned near have to be if you're a catcher. But Dickie was the best catcher I'd ever had—except for my brother, Rick.

I struck out Tony Foster, the third man in Durham's order, getting him to lunge for a change-up out of the strike zone after I'd gotten two quick strikes on him. On my way back to the dugout, I glanced up in the stands and saw Laura jumping up and down and cheering as if I'd just struck out Babe Ruth with the bases loaded.

Neither team did much through the first three innings. Bobby Sutter got the only hit, a single sliced to the opposite field, but he was left stranded at first when Dickie hit a lazy fly ball to left.

I gave up a double with two out in the fourth, but I got Darryl Jackson, Durham's dangerous number four hitter, to fly out to center field for the last out of the inning.

We scored a run in our half of the fourth on a wicked line shot over the right center field wall.

When I got to the mound in the fifth inning, twilight had left the blue sky streaked with swatches of pink. The temperature had dropped a few degrees, and a breeze blew toward the light standards in right field. The wind felt cool against my skin.

Pitchers often talk about the fine line between having too much and not enough, that feeling of magic and power when you have complete confidence in all your pitches; when you're "Rembrandt," painting the corners of the plate, staying along its black edges, dipping inside and outside, just beyond the reach of the frustrated hitters. Such a small line, a matter of an inch or two, yet that distance was literally a difference of miles, the difference between New York City and Norfolk, the difference between one thousand dollars a month and one hundred thousand a month. Inches.

I was "Rembrandt" now, completely focused, almost hypnotic as I got the sign from Dickie, took a deep breath, went into the windup, and let each pitch go. Rhythm, Repetition. Throw to the mitt. Play catch. We didn't score any more runs, but we didn't need to score. I gave up a one-out single in the sixth and another in the ninth.

Johnny Desmond came out to the mound along with Dickie Moore. Our closer, Eric Whelan, was warming up in the bullpen.

"How do you feel?" Johnny asked.

"Like I want to finish."

"He's still hummin', Coach," Dickie said. "Up to me, I'd let him finish."

"It ain't up to you, Dickie."

"Right, Coach," Dickie said and spit out a mouthful of saliva.

"Let me finish, Des," I said.

Johnny Desmond looked around at the crowd, then over at the Durham dugout, then back at me. He tugged at the belt just below his ample belly. "Tell you what. You get Foster, I'll let you pitch to Jackson. Otherwise, I'm comin' out to get you."

"Fair enough." I stood off to the side of the mound and rubbed up the baseball while Johnny returned to the dugout and Dickie set up behind the plate. I heard the murmur of the crowd for the first time since the early innings, heard their anticipation as Tony Foster stepped up to the plate. I thought of Laura for a moment and then chased her from my mind. I had to concentrate.

Rios, Durham's number two man, was on first following his single in the hole between short and third. He had good speed, but I had a good move to first. I figured he wouldn't risk a steal down a run with one out in the ninth, and his number three and four men due up, but I still threw over to first base once to hold him close.

I got one quick strike on Foster and then fell behind two balls and one strike, my last pitch just missing the outside corner, although I could tell that Dickie thought it was a strike by the way he held the pitch for an extra second, as if to give the umpire a chance to change his mind.

In every ball game there were certain times when one pitch or one hit could change the whole complexion of the game, shift the momentum and carry one team to victory. This was one of those times. If I fell behind Foster three balls and one strike, I'd have to come in with a strike or face Darryl Jackson, the league's leading home run hitter, who was on deck. Actually, I wouldn't be facing Jackson—Eric Whelan, our closer, would—but I didn't want Johnny Desmond to pull me.

Tony Foster was hitting .320 and was not the kind of hitter you wanted to fall way behind on, especially in the late innings with the game on the line. The scouting report said that Foster liked fastballs up in the zone. I didn't want to get into the position of having to throw him one.

When I set myself on the pitching rubber and peered in at Dickie, I was surprised to see him giving me the sign for a curve ball. If I missed with this pitch, I'd have to come in with a fastball on the next. So I did something I hadn't done the whole ballgame. I shook him off.

Dickie gave me the same sign again. I shook him off again, and Foster, tired of waiting, stepped out of the batter's box and began loosening his neck and back muscles like a weight lifter. Dickie raised his mask, spit, glared at me, and silently mouthed, "Throw the fuckin' pitch."

Foster stepped back into the box, cocked his bat, gave me an icy stare, and waited.

Dickie squatted, put two fingers down for the curve ball, and set up his target on the inside part of the plate.

Gripping the laces of the baseball, I took a deep breath, went into the stretch, looked over at Rios on first, brought my front leg up and drove my body forward off my back leg, releasing the ball, watching as it sailed toward the center of the plate and then dove inward.

Foster, having already stepped into the pitch and started his swing, hesitated. Surprise showed in his eyes as he realized at the last second that it was not the fastball he expected, but a breaking ball. He tried to hold up, but his momentum carried him forward. The ball clunked off the end of his bat and hopped right back to me on two bounces.

I spun around and threw toward second base, where Bobby Sutter was waiting, but in my haste, I didn't get a good grip on the ball, and it tailed away from Bobby, pulling him off the bag too soon to force Rios. By the time Bobby set himself and threw to first, Foster had already crossed the bag. There were now two men on with Darryl Jackson coming up.

Shit.

Dickie Moore was the first one to the mound. "Helluva pitch," he says.

"Helluva call, Dickie."

He grinned. "You gotta have gonads to play this game, partner. Remember that."

"I blew it. The game should be over."

"Whelan will get 'em."

"Tough break," Johnny Desmond said as I handed him the ball and left the mound to a nice ovation, which wouldn't mean a thing if we lost the game because I made a poor throw to second on a sure double play. I looked up into the stands as I walked off the field and saw Laura waving, blowing me a kiss.

In the dugout my teammates congratulated me on my effort and shook my hand. I put on my warm-up jacket and hoped that Eric Whelan could get the next two hitters. Everyone in the dugout and the capacity crowd of nearly 12,000 were on their feet in anticipation of the upcoming battle between Whelan and Jackson.

Whelan's first pitch was a sinkerball that didn't sink, and Jackson hit it four hundred feet to dead center over the fence. Whelan got the next two hitters on groundouts, but the damage was done. Durham brought in their closer in the bottom of the ninth, and we went down in order.

In the locker room, everyone was in a somber mood. We were two games out of first place again. Radios were silent. The press gathered around my locker, and I gave them the necessary clichés as I sat on a stool, icing down my left arm.

"I felt strong all the way. I'm not second-guessing Johnny Desmond for taking me out. We've got to take one game at a time. I should've made sure of one out instead of trying to rush to get two. If the Mets call me up, I'll be ready." Ad nauseam.

Finally, I got into the shower, toweled off, and dressed. I saw Johnny Desmond on my way out of the locker room, relaxing in his office, feet up on his desk, puffing on a cigar, talking to a reporter.

"Nice game, kid," he hollered as I walked by the door.

"Thanks, Des."

I found Laura sitting in the stands behind the dugout, looking out onto the still-lighted field, watching the groundskeepers as they dragged and raked the infield, smoothing out the rough spots like sculptors working a piece of clay. She sat with her knees up, her arms around them, her chin resting on her kneecaps. I sat down beside her.

"You were wonderful, Michael." She put a hand on my chin and turned my face toward her and kissed me gently on the mouth.

We had kissed hundreds of times, and still I felt something stir inside me each time I kissed her.

"I love to see you in your uniform," she said. Her eyes had a dusting of blue shadow, and her teeth shone white behind lips that were red and glossy.

"We should've won. I can't believe I made such a poor throw to second."

The wind had changed direction, and it blew in from the sea, leaving a hint of salt in its wake.

"I can't help thinking that in two days I'll have to get on a plane and fly home," she said, "and we won't see each other again for a long time."

"I've made that play a hundred times. Two hundred. I could make it in my sleep."

"I suppose I could stay, Michael, if I didn't have one more year of work on my doctorate. But then I've had one more year on my doctorate for two years now. I keep finding other things to do. More important things. Like traveling. Reading. Watching you play baseball."

I was coming off a high from the adrenaline rush I got whenever I pitched, and my nerve endings still felt wired, though my mind felt calm and relaxed. I was acutely aware of the emptiness of the stadium, the sputter of the outfield sprinklers, and the baying of a distant dog.

"I can't let one game bother me. If things keep going the way they are, and I have a good spring training, I'll be in New York with the Mets next summer." I looked out at Harbor Field and imagined what it would be like to be pitching in Citi Field in New York in front of nearly 42,000 people.

"I wish we could be together," Laura said. "We seem so far apart."

Overhead, the moon was in its last quarter, a wafer-thin wedge of light eaten by shadows.

"Maybe you should find someone else," she said.

"What?"

Laura stretched out her legs, rested her heels on the seat in front of her, and folded her hands in her lap. "I don't want to be a distraction," she said, looking down at her hands.

"A distraction? I love you. Remember that."

A few rows up in the stands, a man picked up trash and put it into a large plastic bag.

"You shouldn't have to worry about me back in Minnesota, Michael. You have to concentrate on your career."

"This doesn't sound like you, Laura."

She shrugged. "I guess I've got the blues."

"Everyone gets the blues."

"But not like me, Michael. Not like I get the blues."

"I'm sorry, honey. My mind is still on the game. It ticks me off that we lost. If I'd made a decent throw to second, we'd have won."

"You didn't give up the home run, Michael."

"I know. But dammit, anyway."

Suddenly, we were shadowed in darkness.

"The lights," she said.

"The grounds crew is about done. We've got to go."

"Now? Do we have to go now?"

"Yes." I stood.

Laura grabbed my hand. "Michael."

"Yes?"

She didn't respond.

"What?"

"I wanted to talk."

"We've got to go before they lock up. You don't want to be locked in, do you?"

"No. We'll go now."

I took her in my arms and kissed her deeply, loving the taste of her mouth and tongue.

She held on to me and whispered in my ear. "I love you so much, Michael."

I kissed her ear and gave her a final squeeze. "Take my hand, honey. Watch your step."

"Do you know the way, Michael?"

"Yes. Hold on to me. We'll be fine."

Chapter 8

I push the memory of that day with Laura out of my mind and go to the kitchen in my apartment, open a cupboard, and take out a box of Kraft macaroni and cheese. Now that Jack Stone has offered me a teaching position for next fall, I can consider splurging on the deluxe package of macaroni. Lately, I have been visiting bars during happy hour, where I can eat the free hors d'oeuvres for the price of one beer. Problem is, I usually have trouble stopping at one.

I have just poured the noodles into a pot of boiling water when my cell phone rings, startling me. The name and number on the caller ID cause me to hesitate before I answer.

"Hello, Michael."

I resist the impulse to disconnect. "Hello, Nicole."

"Is something the matter? You sound upset."

"No. I'm not upset. Just surprised."

"Surprised? Why should you be surprised to hear from me? You know how I feel about you."

"Yes. I know."

"I miss you, Michael. I need to see you. Soon."

I can't think of anything to say.

"Michael?"

"Yes?"

"Did you hear what I said?"

"I heard."

"Tomorrow night is Jack's poker night," she says with anticipation in her voice.

"Tomorrow night's Tuesday," I reply, thinking of Pam and what she would say if I canceled our date.

"Yes. So?"

"I've made other plans."

"Well, change them."

"I can't, Nicole."

"Are you saying you don't want to see me anymore? Is that what you're saying?"

"No. You don't understand."

"I think I do understand, Michael. It's perfectly clear."

"What's clear?"

"You're tired of me. I knew it would happen sooner or later."

"I'm not tired of you."

"You don't have to lie to me, Michael."

"I'm not lying. I'm telling you the truth."

"You still find me attractive?"

I hear the sound of her breathing, slow and steady. "Yes, I still find you attractive."

"I know you're seeing someone else besides me. I know that."

"Nicole, I—"

"It's okay. You're young. Good-looking. You could have lots of women. Younger women."

"Age has nothing to do with it."

"You can be honest with me, Michael."

"I am being honest with you."

"Then why won't you see me?"

"I didn't say I wouldn't see you."

"That's what you said."

"If I said that, I'm sorry."

"I'm sorry, too. Tuesday is our night. It's always been our night. You know that."

"And I also know that we can't continue to go on like this. Sooner or later Jack's bound to find out."

"Why are you being so paranoid all of a sudden?"

"Because I've finally got something to lose."

"What are you talking about?"

"Nothing. Forget it. Look, why can't we meet somewhere for a drink?"

"Don't be silly, Michael. What if someone saw us?"

"Right. Why not come to my place? It's always your place or a hotel. I do have a place."

"Jack has his pickup, and the Audi is in the shop."

"Oh."

"Please, Michael. I need to see you. To talk."

"Just to talk?"

"Yes."

"All right."

"Tomorrow night?"

"Okay, Nicole. I'll see you Tuesday night."

*　　*　　*

The radio next to my bed clicks on. It's six a.m. Tuesday morning. I lie still, listening to mellow jazz, thinking that it would be best if I pull up the sheets and remain in bed all day. I wish that I could call three subs: one to fill in for me today at school, two others to fill in for me tonight at Pam's and Nicole's.

After a hot shower followed by a blast of cold water, I feel more willing to face the day. My Chevy coughs and sputters a few times on the way to school. As I pull into the teacher's lot, I wonder how much longer the car will last.

The school building seems oddly quiet. A few students mill around the halls and sit in the cafeteria eating a nutritious breakfast of Coke and nachos. In the faculty lounge, teachers carrying mugs with cute little sayings emblazoned on the sides wait stoically for their fix at the coffee machine.

In my mailbox I find an announcement concerning Kate Fleming's funeral arrangements and a note from Ted Bruder. He wants to see me first thing this morning. Bruder's name triggers my memory. I realize that I haven't spoken to him yet about Danny O'Brien's English final. I hurry out the door of the faculty lounge and down a corridor towards his room.

Half the building—the half I teach in—still has radiators and wood floors. The small student lockers range in color from gray to yellow to rust. Some of the ceilings have been lowered to hide the overhead ducts and pipes and, rumor has it, asbestos.

Ted Bruder's room is located in the newer section of the school, built in the late sixties to accommodate the baby boomers. The floors are tiled, and vents in the floor supply the heat.

Bruder is sitting in a chair, hunched like a question mark over two neat piles of papers on his desk. He wears a vested suit and a pair of half-glasses on the end of his sharp nose. His brown hair is cut close enough to be called a crew cut, but he combs it straight forward instead of back and plasters it down with oil that gives him very short bangs.

I watch as he takes a paper from the stack on his right, looks it over, then, with a flourish, marks it with the red pen in his left hand and places it on the other stack, pausing to make certain that the papers beneath are not disturbed. He hooks his left hand around as he writes, so that he appears to be writing backward.

As I stand outside his door, considering whether to knock or to walk right in, he looks up. "Ah, it's you." Bruder always addresses me as "you" or "say," as if I'm some nonentity.

I nod and enter. I met Ted Bruder the first week of school when he handed me a card that said I could have all my teacher association dues taken out of one check or spread them out over half the year. "You wanted to see me."

"I most certainly did." Bruder pushes himself away from his desk and stands, all 5' 7" of him. "It's about that student of yours. O'Brien."

"Student of ours. And his name's Danny."

"Yes, well . . . anyway, O'Brien came to my room last night after school. He wanted to know if I had spoken with you about reading the final test to him."

"Danny came to see you after school?"

"That is what I just said. Naturally I told him that I had not spoken with you."

"That's great. Why can't you give the kid a break?"

"Because it is tantamount to cheating." Bruder turns away and begins taking more papers out of a briefcase on the floor, stacking them like sandbags around his desk.

"Look," I say, coming at him from another angle, "you know Danny's dyslexic; you know how slowly he reads, how long it takes him. If you won't let me read the test to him, why not agree to give him some extra time?"

"I have allowed you to help him all year." Bruder doesn't look at me but continues stacking papers.

"And I appreciate it," I reply, straining to keep the sarcasm out of my voice. "So why not the final?"

Bruder looks up. "I'll tell you why not the final. Because it is time for Mr. O'Brien to stand on his own. Unless you plan on tutoring him for the rest of his life."

I have a sudden urge to grab Bruder by his bangs and pound his face into the desktop. Instead I say, "Danny's got a chance for a hockey scholarship to the University of Minnesota. But he could lose it if his grades are too low."

"That is not my concern at the moment."

"Just what is your concern?"

Bruder stares at me with no emotion in his face. Then he says, "Getting my papers corrected. Now if you'll excuse me."

"So that's it."

He gives a firm nod.

"You know something, Bruder?"

"What?"

"You're a genuine asshole."

I walk out of the room and down the hall, the wood floor squeaking like an old rocker with each step. I want to believe I didn't hit Ted Bruder because he's much smaller than me. But truth be told, if Jack Stone hadn't offered me Kate Fleming's position, I probably would have acted on impulse and decked Bruder anyway. My angry reaction doesn't surprise me. It's the only emotion besides dread I have been able to generate lately.

As I approach my classroom, I see a figure slouched against the door.

"Hello, Mr. Collins."

"Hello, Danny." Red hair slicked with water, Danny O'Brien stands with his hands scrunched in his jean pockets. "What are you doing here so early?"

"I didn't go home last night."

"You've been out all night?"

"I stayed with a friend. I walked to school this morning."

"Why?"

He shrugs. "I just didn't feel like going home, that's all."

I fumble in my pockets for my room keys. "Come on in and sit down. I'll give your mom a call. She must be worried."

"You didn't talk to Mr. Bruder yesterday," Danny reminds me, disappointment dripping from each word.

"I talked to him this morning."

His face lights up. "You did? That's great, Mr. C. I knew I could count on you."

I hesitate, hold the key in the lock, and look at Danny.

"Bruder said no, didn't he?"

"Let me try again. I'll talk to Jack Stone—"

"No," Danny replies matter-of-factly, shaking his head. "But thanks for trying, Mr. C." He heads down the hall, hands still in his pockets.

"Listen, Danny." I start walking after him, and he breaks into a trot, weaving in and out of the students who are mingling in the halls, opening their lockers.

"Wait!" I call as Danny exits the building at the end of the corridor. The door bangs shut and locks behind him.

Chapter 9

Danny O'Brien is well liked by his peers and most of his teachers. Considered by coach Buzz Thompson "the hardest working kid I've ever coached," Danny has made all-conference and all-state his senior year in hockey. He's bright (his IQ is 120), though he reads at an eighth-grade level. His father is a professor at the University of Minnesota; his mother teaches algebra at Seaton High School. They divorced when Danny was seven.

It's unusual to call someone with an above-average IQ an overachiever, but Danny's learning disability is a wound that requires constant attention, and one that will mend only with prolonged and consistent effort. Though his SAT scores are below average in language, his math scores rank near the top. He has extraordinary comprehension, but he ponders over every word of text. Given his motivation, he'll probably do well in college—if he passes Ted Bruder's English final and receives his scholarship.

I call Mrs. O'Brien at Seaton High School right after Danny leaves the building and explain the situation to her. I reassure her that everything will be fine, that Danny will turn up soon, though I don't feel very reassured myself. Like Danny, Mrs. O'Brien sounds frustrated and upset. Not at me particularly, but at that insensitive giant known as "the system."

"Someone's going to pay for this," she says and hangs up the phone.

As I listen to the silence of the broken connection for a moment, wondering who that "someone" might be, I remember the time last fall when both the O'Briens came to Wilson for parent conferences. It was the first time I'd met Danny's father. While I went over Danny's reading scores with Mrs. O'Brien and talked about Danny's opportunities and expectations after high school, Mr. O'Brien sat by himself at a table and graded papers from his students at the university. Not once did he comment on Danny or ask any questions about his son's progress.

I spend the first three hours of the day gazing at the tops of my students' heads as they peer intently down at their tests like monks bowed in prayer. Time drags. Rather than watch the hands move slowly around the clock face, I would have preferred to be teaching.

In the last two years I've noticed that idleness too often leads my mind from its comfortable island of isolation toward the painful shores of self-scrutiny. Each journey leaves me feeling more lost and confused, as if I'm swimming upstream against a stiff tide. And so I've retreated after each failed attempt to the security of my island, distancing myself from the dangerous riptides of a relationship. I don't want to hurt Nicole any more than I want to hurt Pam, yet there seems to be no way to avoid the treacherous undercurrents in the channel. And maybe by attempting to avoid them, I have only made things worse.

The bell ending the sixth period of the day startles me. Students drop their test booklets and answer sheets on my desk on their way out of the room. As I gather them into a pile, I see Mac Tyler's imposing figure standing in the doorway.

"Come on in. Don't be shy, Mac."

"You ever known me to be?" he replies, sauntering up the center aisle.

I laugh and sit down in the chair behind my desk.

"Congratulations."

"You heard Jack Stone offered me Kate's position?"

"There are very few secrets around here."

"Thanks, Mac."

"You don't sound too thrilled," he says as he squeezes his large frame into a student desk in the front row. He lets his long legs stretch out into the aisle, both legs on the same side of the desk.

"The school board has to approve it."

"That's just a formality as long as Jack's behind you."

"There's also that other matter."

He raises his eyebrows. "Nicole?"

I nod. "I've got to resolve that. I can't have it hanging over my head any longer."

"When do you plan on taking care of it?"

"Tonight. It's Jack's poker night."

"You really think it's a good idea to go over there?"

"No. But this is it. This is the last time."

"The last time."

"Yes. This is it. I'm through with it."

"What about Nicole? Is she through with it?"

"She'll have to be. It's over. I'm going there to tell her."

"Seems foolish to risk it."

"I've got to tell her. I owe her that."

"You owe her? What do you owe her?"

"An explanation."

"Ever hear of the phone?"

"She said she wants to see me."

"Oh."

"It'll be okay, Mac. Besides, I've got other problems to worry about. Ted Bruder won't let me read his final test to Danny O'Brien. And if Danny doesn't pass English, he might lose his hockey scholarship."

"Good old Bruder."

"Got any suggestions?"

"I suppose I could go down to Bruder's room and threaten to kick his ass," Mac says with a laugh.

"I appreciate the offer. But you'd end up in trouble."

"Might be worth it."

"It might be."

"Don't suppose there's any chance Bruder will change his mind?"

"It doesn't look like it."

"So?"

"So my main concern right now is locating Danny. He ran out of here this morning, and he hasn't come back."

"You talk to his mother?"

I nod.

"He'll turn up."

"I don't know. I'm worried."

"You call the police?"

"And tell them what? One of my students didn't show up for finals? Unless Danny's declared a missing person, I doubt the police will do anything."

Mac crosses his arms and leans back in the desk. "How tight is Danny wound?"

"What do you mean?"

"I mean, is he a threat to himself or to anyone else?"

"I don't think so. He's a little high-strung, that's all."

I stand and walk to the bank of windows along the wall. From here I can see a bulldozer and a crane and wrecking ball sitting like giant vultures atop two flatbed trailers next to the parking lot. Beyond the lot are the tennis courts and football field, its grass a bright green courtesy of all the recent rain. *Next year a new school, a new job, and a fresh start.*

"Remember last winter?" Mac says. "When we played Seaton in hockey?"

I turn toward Mac. "What about it?"

"That's the game Danny O'Brien got tossed out of for hitting that Seaton defenseman in the head with a stick."

"I remember. The defenseman had crossed-checked Danny from behind."

"That doesn't justify what Danny did to him. He has quite a temper when you push him into a corner."

I lean against the radiators that run the length of the wall under the windows. The pipes feel cool now, like the touch of a reluctant love. "What are you getting at, Mac?"

"Maybe nothing. I just sense that passing this test means a whole lot to Danny O'Brien. And he might feel Bruder's blind-sided him just like that Seaton defenseman."

* * *

I walk down to the lounge on my free period and check my mailbox. On my way back to my room, Jack Stone stops me in the hall.

"I got a complaint about you from Ted Bruder," Jack says. "He claims you called him an asshole in front of students."

"There were no students around."

"Then you did call him an asshole."

I give a reluctant nod. "Did he tell you why?"

"No."

I explain Danny O'Brien's situation to Jack.

"Apparently," Jack replies, "O'Brien got into it in the parking lot with another student, Chuck Wade, when he left here this morning."

"Wade is always looking for trouble."

"So is O'Brien—lately. I had him in my office last week for mouthing off to Ned Fowler during physical education class."

"This is all Bruder's doing. Why does he have to be so inflexible?"

"Inflexible or not, that's still no reason to use the kind of language you did. I can't have my staff talking like that to one another. Especially in front of students."

"There weren't any students around. It was before school."

"Bruder says there were. And he's demanded that you apologize."

"What students? What are their names?"

"Look, Collins, if it were strictly up to me, I'd let it go. But you know how Bruder is. He's the union steward. He'll push this incident all the way to the superintendent if he has to. Being as you're considered a first-year teacher with no tenure, and I've offered you a position here . . ." Jack Stone shrugs and leaves it at that.

Chapter 10

The headline in the Extra section of the evening paper reads: WHY MEN ARE SUCH JERKS. According to the article, seven out of ten women are worth getting to know and only three out of every ten men. All the good men are either married or gay. *Swell,* I think.

Jerks leave the toilet seat up, leave dates at the door with empty promises, and leave altogether after months of dating without even an explanation. I don't leave the toilet seat up. I wonder if I still qualify.

The article quotes an organization based in San Francisco and New York that focuses on the immutable differences between the sexes. This organization suggests that women really don't care what men feel, and if men tried to tell them, women wouldn't understand anyway. Men who try to become more sensitive to please women are no longer jerks, but wimps. And women ultimately resent wimps who conform to their desires and needs even more than they resent jerks. Despite protestations to the contrary, women actually want men who are wild, adventurous, and unpredictable. Supposedly, the ideal man is a combination of Clint Eastwood, Mahatma Gandhi, and Curly of the Three Stooges.

The article on jerks reminds me of Ted Bruder. My gut reaction is to let Bruder bring his charge before the administration. Then again, since I have no tenure, that idea is nearly as intelligent as telling Jack Stone that I'm sleeping with his wife.

It's 5:00 p.m. I hope my talk with Pam will take less than an hour. Jack usually leaves for his poker game around 7:30. I can be at Nicole's a little after 8:00. But I keep thinking of Murphy's Law, of all that can go wrong.

Hunger gnaws at me, so I trudge into the kitchen and open the refrigerator door. There is one carton of orange juice, leftover macaroni, a half-empty jar of Jif peanut butter, three slices of whole wheat bread, a six-pack of Coke, and a package of hot dogs I'm saving for a special occasion. I spread the Jif over the three slices of bread, eat them, and wash them down with a glass of orange juice. I'm on a health kick.

I leave my apartment at 6:00 and drive across town to the Lakeside Mortuary for Kate Fleming's wake. A number of old mansions in Dakota Lake have been converted into mortuaries. I suspect they're all the same inside, from the thick draperies and carpets to the chandeliers and high-ceilinged rooms, where the wealthy once partied and hoped that money might somehow save them from this ultimate fate.

Less than a dozen people are at the wake when I arrive, and most of them are members of Kate's family. I'd have felt less conspicuous, less uncomfortable, had I arrived later, when there would have been considerably more mourners, but I have little choice if I'm to be at the Stones' house by eight.

I express my condolences to Kate's husband, John. The small, brown-haired man stands stiffly beside his wife's open casket. His brown eyes are glazed, his movements mechanical. He appears to be on the verge of a breakdown.

"Thank you for coming," he says in a voice that sounds preprogrammed.

It would be impolite to leave quickly, so I stand in a corner next to a large wreath on an easel. I still feel guilty about being offered Kate's job, though I know she liked me and considered me her friend. Hell, she would have wanted me to accept it.

As I avert my eyes from the open casket, I wonder who besides my family would come to my wake; who else would really miss me? Pam? *Probably not after tonight.*

I've never thought much about my own death, but now seems as good a time as any. I'd rather be cremated, preferring that my family see my ashes, not my corpse, no matter how skillful the mortician. I wonder who would deliver my eulogy? What would they say? Loving husband and father? That was out. Charitable businessman and beloved member of the community? Not a chance. Impoverished jerk? That sounds closer to the truth.

Would Laura come to my funeral? How would she feel about my death? I picture her weeping uncontrollably over my ash-filled urn.

"Hello, Michael." Beth Stanton's voice brings me back to the present.

"Hello." Beth wears her ash blonde hair up, a dark blue dress, and blue flats.

Looking off toward Kate's casket, she says, "I can't believe this is happening, Michael. Kate was so . . . alive." Her voice cracks, and I believe for a moment that she's going to cry.

I don't know why I suddenly remember that I still owe Beth money for Kate's flowers, and I have only five dollars in my wallet. It isn't that I don't plan on contributing. I just don't get paid till Friday, and I want to eat something besides peanut butter and bread between now and then.

"My mother died unexpectedly last year," Beth says, looking at me now.

"I'm sorry."

"Do you still have your parents, Michael?"

"Yes, I do."

"You're lucky." She dabs her eyes with a Kleenex. "I'm afraid we really don't know much about each other, Michael, even though we've worked together for nearly a year. You're very quiet and within yourself. Were you always that way?"

I feel blood rushing to my face.

"I'm sorry if I embarrassed you. I didn't mean to."

"Don't worry about it. I'm a little out of practice talking about my feelings."

"Most men are."

"Ouch."

"I didn't mean to be critical."

"Is it difficult for women to understand why men aren't as open as women?"

"Not hard to understand. To accept."

More mourners arrive; students and teachers and relatives, and the room becomes crowded.

"Do you believe in an afterlife, Michael?"

"I haven't thought much about it. How about you?"

"Oh, yes. If there isn't another life, a heaven, what would be the point of life here on earth?"

"Does there have to be a point?"

She looks at me as if she thinks I'm kidding.

"I was only thinking out loud, Beth."

"What religion are you?"

"My family never attended church when I was young. My father lost whatever faith he had in God and most of mankind in Vietnam."

"I was raised Catholic," she says, "but I can't accept some of the church's teaching. Especially the way they treat women. So I go to a Free Church now. We accept everyone."

"That sounds reasonable."

"If I tell you something else, Michael, will you promise not to laugh?"

"Sure."

"I think I'm psychic. I sense things."

"Like how?"

She hesitates. Then she says, "Never mind. I hope you get Kate's job."

I wonder if I should tell her that Jack Stone has already offered me Kate's position—or if she already knows. Then I reconsider. It might be better to wait and let Jack handle it, whether she knows or not.

"Thanks, Beth. I hope you get it, too."

She smiles. "No, you don't. Not really."

*   *   *

As I back my Chevy out of a space in the mortuary parking lot, Jack Stone's pickup pulls in beside me.

Jack motions for me to stop and roll down my window. "You're here early," he says, coming around the front of the pickup toward me.

"Thought I'd miss the rush."

Nicole steps out on the passenger side of the pickup and shuts the door. She's wearing a black dress and spiked heels. She glances at me for a moment, her pale skin accentuating the redness of her lips. Then she heads for the mortuary entrance, her heels clicking against the tar surface of the lot.

Jack places both of his large hands on the roof of my car above the driver's side window, leans down and says, "Got plans tonight?"

"No!" I reply emphatically.

"Well, I do. My poker night."

My heart thumps like a flat tire on pavement. Behind Jack a steady stream of cars drives into the parking lot.

"You know," he continues, "I almost decided not to play poker tonight. I mean, what the hell's the point?" He makes a sweeping motion with his right hand, indicating the mortuary. "We're all going to end up here eventually, right?"

I nod.

"But my wife says to me, Jack, it'll do you good to relax. Get your mind off school. Hell, getting me out of the house will probably do her some good, too, don't you think?"

"How would I know?"

Jack bends down closer to my open window. "Something besides Kate's death bothering you, Collins?" he asks in a concerned voice. The lapels on his dark suit flap like angel's wings in the wind.

"Mortuaries make me uncomfortable."

"Me, too." He straightens up, stands quietly for a time with his hands in his pockets, half-turned, and gazes at the mortuary entrance.

I wonder if he's thinking about his dead son.

"You get yourself a sub for Kate's funeral tomorrow, Collins?"

"Not yet."

"Make sure you call in. She worked with you. Best that you go."

"I will."

"You take it easy tonight," he says, hitching up his trousers.

I force a smile and close the window.

* * *

On the way to Pam's, I try to forget Jack Stone and the sweat that's still running down my back. I concentrate on what I plan to say to Pam, on the speech I have rehearsed so many times before in my mind. But now, the more I repeat it to myself, the sillier it sounds. I'm reminded of Paul Simon's tune, "Fifty Ways to Leave Your Lover."

My mind shifts gears at a stoplight, and I recall my brief conversation at the mortuary with Beth Stanton. I wonder what she meant by telling me she was psychic? Did she really know that Jack had offered me Kate Fleming's teaching position? Or did Beth Stanton know something else, something about Nicole and me? Or am I just being paranoid?

I sit in my Chevy outside of Pam's condo for a minute, listening to the engine idle, staring at the low, gray clouds as twilight settles over the city. Then I take a deep breath, shut off the engine, and get out of the car.

Pam's condominium is located in a modern apartment building about three miles from mine. The grass along the sidewalk is long and damp, the air so humid that even the plastic plant in the huge lobby is drooping. I buzz once. The security door clicks open like a cell door. I walk up the carpeted stairs and down a long, narrow corridor. Pam's door is open. I enter and close it behind me. Swedish ivy, ferns, even a cactus decorates her one-bedroom condo. The sweet smell of eucalyptus scents the air.

I hang my sport coat in the front closet as Pam comes out of the bedroom to the right, dressed in jeans and a white blouse and deck shoes, looking solemn, as if she's on her way to an execution. With her short brown haircut, she seems younger than twenty-seven.

"Would you like a drink?" she says, making no attempt to kiss me in greeting.

"Vodka, if you have it."

"On the rocks?"

"Straight."

I step down into the sunken living room and sit on the soft, rounded couch. Copies of the *Wall Street Journal* are arranged neatly on the coffee table. I think of how often we have kissed sitting here on the couch; how our lovemaking has become more rehearsed, as if following a script. How, as I've grown more disenchanted with the relationship, Pam always has to ask, rather hesitantly, if I want to go into the bedroom. I remember feeling like I was outside my body, watching myself perform, when I made love to her. And I remember looking down at Pam's face in the dim light and seeing Laura's.

Pam brings the glass of vodka and sits down on the couch, leaving a cushion between us. She sips her glass of blush wine and comments on the rainy weather. We've always been good at making small talk, at talking about everything except each other.

"Are you uncomfortable?" she asks suddenly, holding the wine glass close to her lips.

"It shows?"

"Yes."

"Aren't you?"

"A little," she says.

I've never really felt comfortable in a romantic relationship with anyone but Laura. I've never known how to say the things other men seem to be able to say, and I've felt silly trying. Getting a date was never a problem in high school or in college. Women like me well enough. But when it became apparent there would always be an unspoken distance between us, that baseball was my number one priority, they would grow disillusioned and the relationship would end, never in an argument or in tears, but more like a distance runner fading in a race.

I look at the liquor in my glass, at the beige carpet, at the Picasso print of Dora Maar on the wall opposite the couch. The only sound I hear comes from the hallway, the closing of some distant door. I wish Pam had turned on some music.

"What's wrong with us, Michael?"

Her directness catches me off guard. She's always been so passive and indirect, so unlike Laura, really. I recall the speech I've rehearsed. I need a few more drinks, more time. Finally, I force the words out through the tightness in my throat. "It's my fault, Pam."

She looks at me but says nothing.

I've analyzed our relationship too many times for it to make sense anymore. I just don't love Pam. Sometimes it bothers me. But what bothers me more is that since Laura I haven't cared about anyone, not even myself.

"A few years ago something happened to a woman I loved," I say.

Pam nods her head, as if she had half-expected it. "It's okay. It's always been okay."

"No. It hasn't." I'm not sure why, but I want her to be angry with me at that moment.

Her eyes film, and she stares down at the wine glass in her hands.

"What I meant was, I couldn't be with anyone for a long time after Laura. The more I forced it, the worse it was."

Pam looks up at me. "I wish you'd tell me about her, Michael." Her tone is softer now, like her expression.

"What does it matter?"

She turns her head quickly away and stares out the glass of the sliding door that looks down onto the lawn.

"I didn't mean that, Pam. It does matter. I'm sorry."

She continues looking away, holding her glass of wine. Her hand trembles slightly.

"I was in love. I'm afraid I still am."

"Are you still seeing her?"

"No. I haven't seen or talked to her in five years."

Pam faces me again. "I'm confused, Michael."

I stand and walk to the sliding glass door.

"Please try and explain, Michael. You can try." The frustration is evident in her voice.

I drink some vodka. The liquor burns when I swallow, makes my eyes water. "There was a . . . problem."

"What kind of problem?"

"Laura was ill."

"Maybe it will help if you talk about it."

"I don't think so. It's something I have to work out myself." I finish my drink, hoping that the booze will dull the pain, block the memory, though it never has before.

Across the street a lone, dark-haired woman strolls along the sidewalk. I see her clearly even in the settling dusk; see the faded blue of her jeans, the tan of her jacket. She reminds me of the many times I have followed dark-haired women, hoping to glimpse their faces, hoping that one of them will be Laura. I rarely think much about what I might say or do if any of them actually turn out to be her.

"You must have loved her a lot."

I turn and look at Pam. "For a long time I thought I loved her too much. Now I think I didn't love her enough."

"What was she like, Michael?"

I have to think for a minute. What was Laura like? *Like no one I've ever known. Like someone I've always known.* "I'm afraid I'm still too close to her."

"After all this time?"

I nod. Suddenly I feel this incredible sense of sadness, of gloom, as if I'm shrinking inside. I wonder if love will ever again be what I imagined.

"I'm worried about you, Michael."

"Don't be."

"I can't help it. We're friends. We'll always be that, won't we?"

"Yes. Friends. Always."

"Promise?"

"I'm afraid I'm not very good at keeping promises. I'm sorry." I look at the empty glass in my hand.

"Would you like another drink?"

I would've liked about three more, but I tell her I have to go.

Pam stands, takes the glass out of my hand, carries it into the kitchen, and rinses it out in the sink.

I remembered something my father once said to me. *If you don't expect too much out of people, they won't disappoint you.*

I retrieve my sport coat and glance out the sliding glass doors once more, looking for the dark-haired woman who was walking along the sidewalk. She's gone.

"I'll miss you," Pam says. She has tears in her eyes.

I remember the article about jerks in the newspaper. Should I say something to make our parting easier, something I really don't mean?

I take her in my arms and hug her tightly. Then, without a word, I walk out the door.

Chapter 11

A curtain of mist falls as I come out of Pam's apartment building. The wind has calmed, and a thin layer of fog hangs like steam over the lowlands. Traffic humming along the street a block away sounds like the muted roar of distant surf.

I drive slowly along the puddled roads through pools of amber light, preoccupied with the halos that ring the streetlights. The Chevy's wiper blades keep up a steady beat like a metronome. I consider driving on like this forever, driving from place to place, never stopping long enough to get involved with anyone.

I've known for a long time that I dated Pam to stem the tide of loneliness that threatened to drown me on nights such as these; nights when my thoughts so often return to Laura; nights when the sense of loneliness is so strong it's almost tangible. I can't help thinking about her, turning the events of the past over in my mind as I would the parts of a puzzle, trying to fit each piece together in a different way. But, always, the result is the same. There is no way to change the past, no way to go back, and yet the past continues to haunt me.

* * *

"What dress should I choose, Michael?" Wearing only a bra and panties, Laura stood in front of her bedroom closet, sipping a glass of red wine.

"Maybe you should take it easy."

She cocked her head.

"With the wine."

"You think I'll get drunk?"

"Not drunk."

"What then?"

I paused, wondering whether I should say what I was thinking. Outside the window, flakes of snow piled on the sill, and ice formed on the panes.

"What?" she said irritably. "What do you think is going to happen to me if I drink too much?"

"No reason to get upset."

"I'm not upset. I only want to know what you meant by that remark."

"Nothing. Nothing at all."

"You're the one who seems upset, Michael."

"It must be your imagination."

"So now I'm imagining things, is that it?"

"Let's forget I brought it up."

"Maybe I don't want to forget it."

"Please, Laura. Just hurry and get ready. The Fords are here."

She peered at the dresses in her closet, fingering each one delicately like they were priceless heirlooms. Suddenly lost in thought, she appeared completely oblivious to my presence. This peculiar tendency to withdraw had increased in frequency and intensity in recent days. One minute she was animated and completely engaged in conversation. The next minute it was as if the conversation had never happened.

I was about to remind her again to hurry when she set the wine glass on the chest of drawers and smiled at me. "I hate it when we fight, Michael. I'm sorry. See, no more wine."

"All right."

"I love you," she said.

I turned and walked out of the bedroom door and down the stairs.

Cameron and Monica Ford were seated on the wicker couch in Laura's living room.

"You'd think Laura was dressing for the prom," I said, trying to make light of the situation but unable to shake a feeling of dread.

Cameron gave a hearty laugh. He was a professor in the English department at the University of Minnesota and Laura's advisor. "No hurry. By the way, Michael, I saw you working out over at the field house the other day."

"Keeping in shape."

Cameron wore a V-neck sweater vest and a corduroy coat with patches on the elbows. His dark hair, tinged with gray on the sides, was cut long enough to suggest he still harbored a trace of liberalism.

"Still working on the old change-up, Michael?"

"Yes."

He nodded solemnly as if to say, *I thought so*. "Perhaps you're not keeping the ball far enough back in your palm before you release it."

"What?"

"Far enough back," he said, trying to demonstrate with an orange he had plucked from a bowl of fruit on the coffee table. "I do have some knowledge of the finer points of the game."

Monica let out a sigh. She was tall and trim, with long legs and short blond hair. The color of her dress nearly matched the dark blue of her eyes. "Is there anything you're not an expert on, darling?" she said with undisguised sarcasm. Monica was a dancer before she met Cameron, having toured with the Joffre Dance Company. Most of her time now was devoted to fundraising for the arts.

Cameron frowned. "Well, I did play some ball in my time."

"Between stints with Chaucer, no doubt," I said.

He hesitated, wondering, perhaps, if I was serious or merely joking. Then his reddish face creased into a widening grin. "Exactly."

"I'll keep the advice in mind, Cameron."

"I could use a drink, Michael," Monica said.

"Martini for me," Cameron said. "Dry."

"Monica?"

"Scotch."

On the way to the kitchen I wondered if inviting the Fords over for drinks had been a good idea. But Laura had insisted. She was Cameron's teaching assistant at one time, and they had remained friends. Still, I had second thoughts as I mixed Cameron's drink, trying to get the right amount of gin and vermouth and then figuring the hell with it.

Lately, Laura had reminded me of Ben Walker. I played double-A ball with Ben at Binghamton. We called him "Fuse" because he was like a firecracker that had been lit and hadn't gone off. No one would room with Ben because of his nightmares, nightmares that left him sweating and shaking in his sleep. We all kept waiting for him to explode. One day he did. A pitcher named Phil Turnblad drilled Ben in the back with a fastball because Ben had homered off him in his previous at bat. Before anyone could stop Ben, he charged the mound and used his bat to fracture Phil Turnblad's skull.

A north wind blew ice crystals against Laura's kitchen window, a sound similar to that of tiny bones breaking. I poured a glass of Scotch for Monica and brought the Scotch and Cameron's martini back to the living room. Cameron and Monica were still sitting on the couch, but their eyes were fixed on the stairs.

As I turned to see what they were looking at, a cold, damp chill ran through me. I nearly dropped the drinks I was carrying.

Laura was standing on the bottom step of the landing—stark naked. Her hands hung limply at her sides. Her dark hair, usually waved, was long and straight, framing a face whose natural olive color had faded like a tan in winter.

I stood rooted to the floor.

"Jesus," Cameron muttered in a voice just above a whisper.

The sound startled me, like an epithet uttered in church. "Laura?" I said, as if I was talking to a stranger. The expression on her face reminded me of a child's, a little girl who had misplaced a favorite doll and was trying desperately to remember where she'd put it. "Laura?" I said again, only louder.

She stared at me and began laughing hysterically.

"My God," Monica said. She stood, grabbed the afghan draped over the back of the couch, and ran to the stairs, wrapping the coverlet around Laura.

Laura continued laughing, throwing her head back, as if it was all a sick joke.

I thrust the cocktail glasses at Cameron, spilling Scotch on my hands, and rushed to Laura. "It's okay," I said, putting my arms around her, drawing her close. "It's okay."

She stopped laughing and began shivering.

I picked her up, cradled her in my arms, and carried her up the stairs and into her bedroom. On her brass-framed double bed lay a half-dozen of her dresses. They had been cut to pieces.

"Michael," Monica called from downstairs. "Is there anything we can do?"

"No. It's all right now. We'll be fine."

"You're sure?"

"Yes."

"You'll call and let us know if—"

"Yes. I'll let you know."

Laura and I sat huddled together on the cool hardwood floor of her room. She fell asleep in my arms as I stroked her hair and rocked her like a father rocking a child frightened by a storm, just the two of us, listening to Cameron and Monica downstairs in the living room as they gathered up their coats and boots and left, pulling the front door shut behind them.

Laura slept for what seemed like a long time before she finally woke.

"I want you to promise me something, Michael," she whispered. Her face was close to mine, and her breath was sweet with a hint of wine.

The house creaked as the winter wind whistled through the cracks. The furnace kicked on, sending waves of warm air through the heating vents.

"I've always taken care of myself, Michael, always been independent. But if I ever get sick, I want you to promise you'll take care of me till I'm well again."

There was part of me that wondered why she would ask this of me, that wondered what price I'd pay if I made this promise. But there was an even larger part of me that would do anything I could to keep us together.

"I promise."

"Mean it, Michael. I want you to mean it. Not just say it." Her voice was full of pain and doubt.

"I do mean it. I promise I'll take care of you."

"Remember," she said, resting her head against my chest.

"I will. Everything's going to be fine." I hugged her and knew she was herself again. "You'll see. We're going to get some help."

"No," she said forcefully and pulled away from me.

"For God's sake, Laura."

"You don't understand, Michael."

"Damn right I don't! Why don't you explain it to me?"

She got to her feet, pulled the afghan around her, and stood for a moment in front of the mirror, staring at her image.

I wondered whom it was that she saw. Then she shuffled over to the bed and sat down, paying no attention to her dresses or to what she'd done to them.

"I didn't mean to get angry, Laura."

She stared blankly at the hardwood floor. "I'm afraid," she said in a whisper, as if to herself.

"It's all right. I'm here."

"You can't protect me from everything, Michael. Not from everything."

"That's why we need help."

She looked at me then. Her eyes had a dark, haunted cast. "But I'm afraid of what the doctors might find."

"And I'm afraid of what will happen if we try to solve this by ourselves."

"It's my mother's fault," she said, anger now evident in her tone.

"What's your mother got to do with this? She's dead."

"No, Michael. She's not dead."

"But you—"

"I told you she died of cancer because I was afraid. Afraid that if I told you the truth, you'd leave me."

"The truth? What truth?"

She gazed out the window at the endless darkness and said, "My mother's in a mental institution, Michael. She's been there for years."

Chapter 12

I force Laura from my mind and concentrate on the Stones' house on the hill, on the downstairs lights glowing behind the curtains in the windows. I don't want to go in, don't want to be here, but a voice inside my head tells me to get out of the car and walk up the steps to the front door. Already this evening I've ended one relationship that has reached a dead end. As I knock, I know it's time to end this one as well.

"You're late," Nicole says, holding open the screen door as I step inside. She's wearing the same black dress she wore to the wake.

"I didn't know what time you'd return from the mortuary," I reply in the way of an excuse.

"You're really not much of a liar, Michael."

"I'll take that as a compliment."

She shuts the front door. "Take it as anything you want. You're still late. We don't have much time."

As she leans forward to kiss me, I turn my head away. "We were just going to talk, Nicole, remember?"

She steps back and gives me a long look. "Tell me what's wrong."

"Wrong? What could be wrong?" I make no attempt to hide the sarcasm. "Doesn't what we've been doing here strike you as wrong?"

"I see." She stares at me for a time; then she heads toward the kitchen, her bare feet sinking into the plush carpet. "I'll get us a drink."

"I don't want a drink."

"Oh, yes you do."

"How the hell do you know what I want?"

Over her shoulder, she replies, "You're here, aren't you?"

I stand in the living room feeling embarrassed by what she's said and angry, too. Unfortunately, there's more than a little truth in what she's implied.

I hear her shut the refrigerator door in the kitchen and the clink of ice cubes dropping into glasses. I might not know much about myself, but I know now that I should never have come here. I need to use the bathroom upstairs. Then I'm leaving for good.

On the second-floor landing, I notice the hallway is dark, save for a strip of light under the door of the room Nicole refused to show me the first time I came to the house. *If Jack's at his poker game, then who . . .* For an instant, I have an urge to run. *Jack's home! It's a setup. That's why Nicole was so anxious for me to come over tonight. It's some kind of devious plot designed by Jack and Beth Stanton to deprive me of Kate Fleming's teaching position . . . Come on, no one's here. Nicole's got as much to lose as you do. Probably more.*

Curiosity gets the better of me. I walk down the hall and turn the knob. The door swings open. I enter and stand in the center of the room.

The air smells of lemon Pledge. A dim light from a gooseneck lamp on the desk casts long shadows on the baseball pennants that are tacked to the walls: Minnesota Twins, Chicago White Sox, Detroit Tigers. A fishing rod and reel stands in one corner and a baseball bat in another. A photo album is open on the bed. I don't have to look at the photos in the album to know whose room this was, but I look anyway.

At first, I think Jack Jr. looks like his father, that he has the potential for the same thick neck and shoulders, the same powerful physique. But as I turn the pages, see him at his birthday party or opening Christmas presents, doing something other than holding a dead pheasant or a stringer of shiny bass, I see Nicole in the boy's face, recognize the look in his eyes, which tells me there's a special bond between mother and son, a bond only they share.

"What are *you* doing in here?"

Nicole's voice startles me. It takes a second for me to realize she has placed the emphasis on the "you," like I'm the last person in the world who should be in this room. "I saw the light."

She hurries over to the bed, bends over, and snaps the photo album shut. "You shouldn't be in here." She picks up the album and clutches it to her chest, as if it's a baby threatened by an intruder.

I retreat a few steps toward the door. "You were up here before I arrived. After you came back from the mortuary."

"What business is it of yours?"

"Why didn't you want me in here?"

She opens her mouth, but no words come out.

Through the window behind her, I see the headlights of cars passing on the street.

I point to the photo album. "Is it because you didn't want me to see that? Because you didn't want me to see this . . . shrine?"

"How dare you!"

I'm angry with her, angry with myself for being here, but I realize I have come on too strong, that I've hurt her. "I'm sorry. That was unkind."

She bows her head and lowers the album, as if holding it requires great effort. She holds it waist high in her hands and says, "It's all I have left. Jack took everything else."

"But your son's death was a tragic accident."

"Jack should never have taken him out on the lake in that weather. Never!" As she raises her head, her face, twisted in bitterness, suddenly appears much older.

"And you can't forgive Jack for it."

"It's not your concern."

"How can it not be?"

"What we have has nothing to do with what happened to my son."

"Doesn't it? And while we're on the subject of us, what exactly do we have?"

"You know."

"Yes. I'm afraid I do." I lean against the doorjamb and put my hands in my jacket pockets. "Jack's offered me Kate Fleming's job next year."

"I'm happy for you."

"Are you happy for me or for yourself?"

"For both of us, Michael."

"I want the job. I need it. If Jack ever finds out I'm sleeping with you, Nicole, I'm finished."

"What about me? What about my needs?"

"I'm sorry about what happened to your son. I'm sorry about what's happened with you and your husband. But most of all, I'm sorry about what happened between us."

"Don't say that, Michael. There's nothing to be sorry about."

"Yes, there is."

Nicole sets the photo album gently on the nightstand next to the bed. She stands in profile, gazing down at it, the black dress clinging tightly, her curves still in all the right places. "I'm in love with you, Michael."

"You don't mean that."

She faces me. "I do mean that. I need you."

As I stare into her gray eyes, eyes that for so long have been devoid of any genuine emotion, I see her longing, feel her pain, and hear the emptiness in her heart. And in those hollow gray eyes, I see my reflection. I know now it isn't an act, that Nicole truly believes she needs me. But need isn't the same as love. I start to leave.

"Wait, Michael!" She rushes toward me and slips her arms around my neck. "Please," she says, resting her head on my chest.

Her blond hair tickles my chin; her soft breasts push against me. Unsure as to what to do with my hands, I let them hang at my sides. "It isn't right, Nicole. It never was. Let it be over. Let it go."

"I can't," she says, her voice strained.

"You've got to talk to Jack. Get this thing between you settled once and for all. Give yourselves a chance. Give me a chance."

Her shoulders shake; her breath comes shorter as she begins to cry. She pushes her face hard against me, muffling her sobs, as her tears dampen my shirt.

I can't believe the tears are all for me—for us. Rather, they're for her son, for Jack, for everything.

Finally, as her crying subsides, she steps back and looks up with red, swollen eyes. "I must look awful."

"No. You look . . . real. For the first time, you look real."

She tilts her head as if to ask what I mean, but suddenly her pupils dilate, and instead of asking, she covers her mouth with her right hand, stifling a gasp.

I turn around.

Jack Stone is standing in the hallway, glaring into the room.

Chapter 13

My eyes are fixed on Jack Stone's large hands. I watch as he opens and closes each, balling them into tight fists.

"Jack!" Nicole says. She still covers her mouth, as if for protection. "We . . ." Abruptly, she stops, realizing that nothing she says can explain away what has happened between us.

Heart pounding, throat as dry as chalk dust, I back away from Jack, wishing I could somehow disappear.

"Jack," Nicole says again more softly, fresh tears streaming down her cheeks. The color drains from her face as she moves stiffly toward him, palms up in a pleading gesture, putting herself between us.

But Jack pushes her aside with a swipe of his hairy arm, like a grizzly brushing away a pesky cub. Then he steps forward and clamps his hands around my throat, crushing my windpipe, wringing the life out of me.

I make no attempt to stop him.

"Jack!" Nicole cries. "Stop! Jack!"

Teeth clenched, hands hard as bronze, Jack Stone continues squeezing.

"Jack!" Nicole yells.

My vision blurs, and I choke. I struggle for air as blood roars in my ears and bizarre images explode in front of my eyes like fireworks in a night sky. My legs buckle. I'm losing consciousness.

Nicole screams.

Suddenly, I'm jerked back and forth, pulled like a doll between two selfish children. One of Jack's hands releases its grip on my throat, then the other. Air rushes into my lungs, and blood surges to my brain with such force I think it'll burst. As my head clears and my eyes focus, I realize I'm lying on the floor coughing, gagging, as if in a fit.

Nicole kneels beside me, brushing the hair away from my forehead. "Michael! Oh, my God, Michael!" she says, over and over again.

It takes awhile before the coughing ceases and my breathing returns to normal. With Nicole's help, I sit up and lean my back against the bed.

"Are you all right?"

I nod and carefully feel my throat, raw now where Jack's nails and thick fingers dug into my skin.

"I tried to make him stop, Michael, to pull him off."

I nod once more. It makes more sense than trying to talk, more sense than most of what I've done this evening.

"Jack went crazy. I didn't know what to do. He's so strong I—"

I place the index finger of my left hand lightly against her lips to quiet her, touch the side of her face, hoping to settle her down. Adrenaline recedes like a tide in my system, and I feel surprisingly calm, composed.

Nicole takes my left hand in both of hers and holds it against her cheek. Blood is lodged under her long fingernails, having been used to wrest Jack's hands from my throat.

"Where's Jack?" I rasp.

"I don't know," she replies, wiping away her tears with the back of a hand. Her eyes suddenly grow wide with panic. "The gun!"

"Gun?" I repeat as my heart kicks into gear again.

"Jack's gun!" Nicole stands and rushes out the bedroom door.

The adrenaline rush jogs my memory. Jack has a gun in the glass case in the den. I try getting to my feet, but my legs won't support the idea, and I sit down again with a thump. I consider crawling under the bed and then, as I picture Jack on his knees, firing a few rounds at me as I cower helplessly, I decide against it.

Nicole returns and kneels beside me with a look of relief on her face. As if making an offering, she holds out both hands and shows me the gun. "I thought Jack was going to shoot you," she says, the panic still evident in her voice.

I gaze at the pearl-handled grip, at the black steel barrel. "Is he still in the house?"

She shakes her head.

I lean my head against the bed behind me and let out a long sigh of relief.

"What are we going to do, Michael?" Tears have left tiny tracks in the makeup on her milky white complexion.

I clear my throat. "You're going to have to decide for yourself what you want to do. All that's left for me to do is finish out the school year . . . and collect my last check."

"Oh, Michael. I'm so sorry. I never wanted this to happen."

"Nothing we can do about it now."

"But what about this?" She nods, indicating the gun.

I shrug.

"Will you take it with you?"

I shake my head.

"Please, Michael. I don't want it in the house. I'm frightened."

"You don't think Jack's going to shoot you?"

"I don't know what he's going to do. He nearly killed you. Please. Take the gun."

"Doesn't he have others in the house?"

"He keeps his hunting rifles at the gun club. Please," she says in an anguished voice. She lowers her hands, lets her chin fall to her chest, and begins crying soft little sobs.

I listen for a time and then, against my better judgment, I say, "Okay, Nicole. I'll take the gun."

* * *

Jack's pickup isn't in the driveway when I walk out to my car. I have no idea what has happened to him or where he might have gone, and that worries me. I consider calling the police and reporting Jack's assault, but I quickly dismiss the idea. The police will want to know what I was doing in Jack's house, what triggered Jack's assault.

The mist has stopped, but the air is still cobweb thick with humidity as I drive away. I open the driver's side window to keep the muggy air from fogging up the windshield and check the dashboard clock. It's 10:00 p.m. I have ten hours till I have to return to school and face Jack Stone again. I glance at the gun resting beside me on the car seat. What would have happened had Nicole not intervened? And what will happen when Jack sees me tomorrow? Will he try again? My hands are shaking. I pull over to the side of the road and try to get control of myself, of my emotions.

As I sit behind the wheel, watching the headlights of the oncoming cars, the beams nearly blinding on this moonless night, I wonder how I let myself become involved with another man's wife, how I could do that to Jack Stone—like him or not —or to anyone, and I hate myself for it. Then I remember Laura, and like a strange shape in a darkened room, another ominous thought forms in my mind. And that thought helps me see for the first time the unavoidable course I have charted for myself, and how I've let the past nearly destroy me.

* * *

Storm clouds towered above me, rising like great columns of black smoke from a distant fire at the edge of the earth. Rumbling thunder reminded me of my childhood and my mother's explanation that thunder was caused by God moving furniture, doing a little housecleaning.

I drove toward the storm, toward Laura's, hoping I could get to her house before the cloudburst. Recently, she'd behaved as if she was in one of her hyper phases, cleaning house at all hours of the night, correcting papers till dawn, baking enough pastries to feed an army, and, through all of this, denying she needed rest or sleep.

I'd been trying to reach her by cell phone for nearly two hours. It was 6:30 p.m. She was supposed to be finished teaching her modern poetry class at the university by 4:00 p.m. I wondered if her cell phone might be off. She sometimes did that when, finally exhausted, she wanted to sleep undisturbed.

Rain spit through the driver's side window. Wind gusts shook branches like they were twigs. Dead leaves swirled in tiny funnels. Thunderheads climbed higher, shrouding the sun. The sky suddenly darkened, as if in an eclipse.

There was darkness behind the windows along the front of her house, and I could hear no sound save the roar of rushing wind and the hammering of my knuckles against the front door. I cupped my hands and peered through the glass, hoping to see something, but soon gave it up when I realized nothing could be heard above the din of the storm. I stood on the porch, hands on my hips, contemplating what to do, telling myself to ignore the anxious feeling that rose like flood water inside me.

On impulse I tried the doorknob and was surprised to find it unlocked. And though I'd been in Laura's house many times before, stepping uninvited into her darkened living room, a room lit only by occasional flashes of lightning, I felt unsure of myself, as if I'd entered an unfamiliar landscape, an alien world filled with strange shapes and eerie silhouettes unrecognizable in the shadows. Wind rattled the glass panes, and thunder muffled my footsteps as I moved in slow motion, pausing after each step, waiting for the next lightning flash to brighten the way as I searched blindly for a lamp or light switch.

Halfway across the living room, I heard another sound in between the cracks of thunder and gusts of wind, a sound not unlike a moan, but was it the moan of wood bending against the force of wind, or was it human? Was it Laura?

The sound was above me, so I turned in the direction of the stairs and stumbled into the coffee table, banging my shin against its hard edge. I swore and stepped around the table, and with hands out in front of me, I felt my way to the staircase, finally grabbing the banister as though it were a lifeline. I groped for the light switch I knew was along the wall, and when my fingers felt the familiar plastic shape, I flicked the switch up and down till it became apparent that no matter how many times I tried, the switch wouldn't work without electricity.

I waited for the next flash of lightning before I ascended the stairs, holding onto the banister for support should I make a misstep. Nearing the top landing, I again heard the moan, only this time I was certain the sound did not come from an inanimate object. I moved down the hall, as the moans grew louder and more consistent, till I came to the bedroom doorway.

I stood still, waiting in the dark, getting my bearings, one hand on each side of the door frame, hearing thunder and wind, and now pellets of rain drumming on the roof and window panes. Between bursts of lightning that lit the bedroom nearly every other second, like flashbulbs at a Hollywood premiere, I saw two figures, Laura and a man on the bed, both of them moaning, he moving up and down on top of her, his movements stuttering, as if I was viewing a motion picture film through an old kinescope, and she with her legs locked around his back in an unmistakable sexual dance of pleasure. In that moment, as I stood rooted to the floor, I felt as if my soul had left my body, never to return.

I looked away and stepped across the hallway and leaned against the wall. I swallowed the bile in my throat and took deep breaths to keep from vomiting. I could still hear their moans, and I cupped my hands over my ears and lurched down the hallway and then the stairs, bumping against the wall on one side and the banister on the other, nearly falling as I reached the bottom step. I stumbled across the living room and out the door to the porch and into the driving rain, where I stood on the sidewalk amidst all the thunder and lightning and let the drops beat down on my face and body and mingle with my tears.

I wept till the deluge washed away my sense of sorrow, till I felt the first flames of anger and betrayal.

Who was he?

I waited.

I waited thirty minutes, sitting in my car, listening as heavy dark particles of rain fell like pieces of coal from the blackened sky. As I waited, I imagined how Laura would react when I finally confronted her, and I pictured different scenes in my mind, trying to settle on one that would give me the greatest satisfaction, on one that would hurt her most.

When the rain let up, he came out the door and down the sidewalk. As he hurried to his car and I saw him clearly, shock sliced my heart like a razor.

It was her advisor, Cameron Ford.

Chapter 14

Jack Stone's pearl-handled gun rests beside me on the car seat. I consider bringing it with me to school for protection and then dismiss the thought as absurd. Perhaps I should toss it out the window, throw it into the lake. But what if some kid, some swimmer finds it? No.

Take it home till you can think more clearly, figure out what to do with it.

A warm wind blows through the open car window. I smell fish and lake water and hear the lapping of waves against dock pilings and crickets chirping. I recall something that Mac Tyler said to me last Friday night at Jack Stone's house.

Sometimes things have to fall apart before you can put 'em together.

I stare at my hands, holding them out in front of me. They're steady now. I put the car in gear again and step on the accelerator.

Halfway home I remember that tomorrow is Kate Fleming's funeral. I won't have to teach school. My relief is quickly tempered by the realization that Jack Stone will probably attend.

I park the Chevy at the curb and walk up the stairs to my apartment with the gun tucked in my belt under my shirt. As I open the door, I flick on the light switch and scan the room in one motion, wondering whether Jack Stone might be lurking behind a chair, looking to finish what he started.

Though the windows are open, the apartment feels warm and stuffy. I turn on the window fan and go into the bathroom and peer at my throat, which is red and tender, as if I have been hanged. I think of ways I can cover the redness left where

Jack Stone's fingers dug into the skin. I would wear a turtleneck sweater if it were winter or a tie if I had one.

Aw, the hell with it. If anyone asks me what happened to my neck, I'll tell him the truth.

No, I won't.

I open the nightstand drawer next to my bed and pull the gun out of my waistband. I'm about to set it down when I realize that I haven't checked to see if it's loaded.

Jesus, it feels awfully heavy.

As I stare at it, unsure as to how to release the magazine, my cell phone rings. The sudden sound startles me. I lurch forward and the gun slips out of my hands. I jump back as it lands with a thud in the open drawer. Sweat beads on my brow as I stand rigid for a moment, waiting for it to fire.

My cell rings three more times before I feel calm enough to answer. My first thought is that it might be Jack Stone calling to see if I'm home. Then, as I read the caller ID, I relax.

"Hello, Mother."

"Sorry to call so late."

I don't know what to say. The silence seems endless.

"How are you?" she asks.

"Fine." *What would she say if I told her my principal had just tried to strangle me? What would she say if I told her I have been sleeping with his wife?*

"You don't sound fine, Michael. Is something the matter?"

"No, really, I'm okay."

"I'm calling to remind you. It's your father's birthday tomorrow. Did you forget?"

"Yes, I did. I've had a lot on my mind lately."

"I suppose, you being so excited about getting a teaching position next year. Have you told Pam?"

"Yes, I told her. Why?"

"Now that you have a full-time job, I thought perhaps that you two might . . ."

"Oh."

"Are you sure there's nothing the matter, Michael?"

"Positive."

"Good, because tomorrow I'm planning a celebration at the house. For Dad and you."

"There's no need to include me, Mother. It's Dad's birthday."

"But after all these years, Michael, you've finally gotten a teaching position. I think that calls for a celebration."

"Nothing's permanent."

"Oh, don't be such a pessimist. Be happy. Be proud of what you've accomplished. You could've given up a long time ago, but you stuck with it. And now it's paid off."

How can I tell her? How can I ever explain?

"Why don't you bring Pam along?"

I should tell her that I'm not seeing Pam anymore, that it's over between us. I should tell her a lot of things. "Sure."

"Seven o'clock. Come early. For a change."

"Okay."

"See you tomorrow, then."

"Good-bye, Mother."

I stare at the phone in my hand, wondering what the hell I'm going to do. I disconnect and shuffle to the bed and sit down, my eyes aimed at the nightstand drawer. My neck feels like it's been buffed with coarse-grade sandpaper.

I pick up the gun and examine it once again. It would be so easy to put the gun to my head and pull the trigger. *Well, maybe not that easy.* Carefully, I set it down and close the drawer.

I call and leave my name and a message on the answering service tape that I'll be attending Kate Fleming's funeral tomorrow and will need a sub. Then I lie down on the bed and close my eyes, too tired all of a sudden to get up and take off my clothes and turn out the light.

I drift off into a restless sleep in which I find myself at Jack Stone's house. Nicole and I are on one side of the front door, holding it closed. Jack is pounding on the other side, demanding to be let in. The pounding becomes progressively louder and is soon accompanied by a voice that doesn't sound at all like Jack Stone's.

I wake with a start and glance at the radio alarm clock on the nightstand. I've been asleep only a half hour. It takes me a moment to realize that someone *is* knocking on my apartment door. I fear that my dream has become reality till I hear the youthful voice.

"Mr. Collins, are you in there?"

I get up and open the door and let him in.

"Hello, Mr. Collins."

"Hello, Danny."

Danny O'Brien rushes into the apartment and runs a hand through his tangled red hair.

"I don't know what to do, Mr. Collins. I need someone to talk to, to help me think." His body, in a perpetual state of twitch, reminds me of a bird's.

I want to tell him that I'll help, that we'll get everything straightened out, but considering the mess I've made of my own life, I'm uncertain that I can. All I can think of to say is, "I'd better call your mother. You've been missing for two days."

"No! Don't call her. Not yet." He gazes apprehensively around the room, as if deciding whether or not to stay. His clothes smell strongly of cigarette smoke.

"All right. Are you hungry?" I ask, hoping that food will help him relax. "Would you like something to eat or drink?"

Instead of answering, he stares at me. "What happened to your neck?"

"My neck?" I stall.

"Yeah. It's all red."

"Sunburn."

"Sunburn? It's been cloudy for days."

"One of those tanning beds."

"Come on, Mr. C."

"You don't buy that, huh?"

He shakes his head.

"Well, that's the best explanation I can come up with at the moment." As Danny continues to stare at my neck, apparently contemplating a more direct question, I change the subject. "How 'bout a hot dog and a Coke? It's my specialty."

"I don't know." His left Nike shoe taps a nervous beat against the floor, keeping time to some inner rhythm.

"It's no problem."

"Okay," he says and then adds, "Could I have two hot dogs?"

In the kitchen, I place two wieners in a pan of water. While I wait for the water to boil, I take a can of Coke out of the refrigerator and bring it to the living room and hand it to Danny.

"Thanks," he says and resumes pacing back and forth.

"Why don't you come out to the kitchen, Danny? We can talk while you eat."

He nods and follows me.

"Catsup or mustard?" I ask as he stands behind a chair at the kitchen table.

"Both," he blurts.

"My kind of guy."

He responds with a crooked little smile and takes a quick swallow of Coke.

"Would you like a glass and some ice?"

He shakes his head.

I'm reluctant to start questioning him about where he's been or what he has on his mind for fear it will turn him off. Better to let him begin when he's ready.

"Sit down, Danny."

He gives a little nod and sits stiffly in the chair, setting the pop can so hard on the tabletop that some of the Coke spills out. He glances up quickly, as if he's just been accused of theft.

"Don't worry. I'm not going to ask you to leave." I wipe up the tiny puddle with a napkin and put a plate and knife on the table along with the catsup and mustard. I let the wieners boil till they puff up, rescuing them from the scalding water with a pair of tongs just before they split, a technique I have perfected through years of practice and hundreds of wieners. I place the wieners in buns and the buns on the plate in front of him.

"Thanks," he says, smothering the hot dogs first with mustard, then catsup.

"Sorry I don't have any chips," I say as he leans forward and begins to wolf down a hot dog.

"'At's all rife," he mumbles with his mouth full.

I get a Coke out of the refrigerator for myself, pop the tab, and sit down in the chair opposite him. The brown hot dog buns are the same color as the freckles covering his face.

When he finishes, he sits back in the chair and pats his belly, as if he's a gourmand who has just eaten a meal at an elegant French restaurant.

"There's more if you like, Danny."

A look comes over him suggesting he's embarrassed by the speed at which he's devoured the food. "Oh, that's plenty, Mr. Collins. Thanks." Catsup and mustard stain the corners of his mouth. "You're a good guy, you know, Mr. Collins."

"A saint."

"No, I'm serious. I mean, you went to bat for me with Bruder."

"It didn't do much good."

"But you tried."

"It's my job. I'm supposed to try."

"Ah, you'd a done it anyway, whether it was your job or not."

"Thanks," I reply, feeling good for the first time all day. "What are your plans now, Danny? How can I help?"

He has one hand in the pocket of his jean jacket while the other fidgets with the Coke can on the table. "Well, I've been thinking that maybe your original idea might not be too bad."

"My original idea? I didn't know I was capable of one."

He stares blankly at me. My attempt at humor escapes him.

"Remember when you said you'd talk to the principal, Mr. Stone?" he continues. "Well, if you talked to him and he talked to Bruder, maybe I could still have the English final read to me."

My heart feels as if it's been run over. "I don't think that's such an original idea anymore."

"Why not?"

"Mr. Stone and I sort of had a . . . falling out."

"How come?"

"It's personal."

"Oh." He gazes across the table, looking as if he's suddenly made a connection between the marks on my throat and the "falling out." Then again, maybe I'm paranoid.

"I tell you what, Danny. If you'll come to school the day after tomorrow, I can read you the finals you missed today."

"Why not tomorrow?"

"It's Ms. Fleming's funeral tomorrow."

"Oh, right."

"And that evening, if you'd like, I can help you study for Bruder's final. I know you can pass it."

He examines the label on the Coke can. "I have to pass it."

"You will."

"If my grades aren't high enough, I'll lose my scholarship."

"There are other schools."

"No." He pushes his chair away from the table, the legs squealing against the tile, and stands up. "I've got to go to the university."

"Okay," I say, trying to settle him down. "I'll help you study. You'll do it."

He runs a hand through his hair. "Can I use your bathroom?"

"Sure. It's off the living room. Which is also the bedroom." I watch him as he hurries out of the kitchen. For eighteen years, his life has been a struggle. All he's ever wanted is to succeed in school so he can play hockey. I wish I could guarantee that someday his life will be better, that passing Bruder's English final will make a difference, that college will make a difference. But if there is one thing I've learned, it's that an education is no guarantee that you won't screw up your life.

I clean off the table, leaving the dirty dishes in the sink. When I enter the living room, Danny is standing in front of the bookshelf, running his hands gently over the book spines. The radio alarm clock on the nightstand reads 1:00 a.m.

"You tired, Danny?"

He whirls around, as though he hasn't heard me enter the room. "No."

"I really should call your mother. Let her know you're okay."

"If you do, I'll leave."

"I don't understand."

"She doesn't either."

"What doesn't she understand?"

He starts to answer and then changes his mind.

I approach the problem from another angle. "You feel she puts too much pressure on you."

"Ha!" he responds. "Just the opposite. She doesn't put any pressure on me at all. She thinks I do just fine. And so does my father."

"So do I, Danny."

"Everyone thinks I do just fine," he says disgustedly, throwing up his hands.

"What's wrong with that?"

"Don't you get it, Mr. Collins? *I* don't think I do just fine. In fact, I know I don't. Look at these books you have here. Any time you want, you can pick one up and read it in a few days. I can't. It takes me weeks. I have to rely on tapes and tutors, on someone summarizing it for me. The only reason I do fine is because I get help. I want to make it on my own."

"You are making it on your own. You're the one who's taking responsibility for your life, the one who's putting in all the effort, taking advantage of the opportunities your athletic ability provides. Besides, your disability is physical and not your fault."

"Be honest with me, Mr. C. I'm never going to read much better, am I?"

"Think of how much your reading has improved these last three years. If you keep working at it, then—"

"I said honest."

"All right. Reading isn't ever going to be easy for you, Danny. In truth, you may never get much better." Having said it, seeing the disappointment in his eyes, I regret it.

"And I'll never be a success like my father, will I?"

"So you may never be a professor at the university. But that doesn't mean you can't be a success at something else."

He slumps in the overstuffed chair, seemingly exhausted by frustration and despair. As he rubs his eyes with the palms of his hands, I notice that the tips of his fingers are raw from chewing his nails.

He looks up at me and says, "I was supposed to be a brilliant student, a doctor or a lawyer, like the sons of my father's asshole friends at the university. When the school psychologist told my father I had a learning disability, he about croaked. For a long time, he didn't believe it. He sent me for private testing, even sent me to a private school for a while. Then he gave up on me. Oh, he said he wanted me to do well. But I could tell he never thought I'd make it. One night I heard my mom arguing with him about how he felt. 'Sooner or later Danny will fail,' he said. Those were his exact words. I'll never forget it. He doesn't care about my hockey playing. It's the academics he's concerned about. He figures I'm going to fail, that it's only a matter of time. My mom told him he needed counseling. But he never went."

"So you're trying to prove to your father that he's wrong."

"Not only him. I'm trying to prove to *me* that he's wrong. And I'm going to do it. Whatever it takes."

I think about my own father and the unresolved hurt and anger that exists between us.

I kneel in front of the chair so that we're at eye level. "You've got to stop putting so much pressure on yourself. You're my best student. I wish all my students were as dedicated as you. But there's a limit. You can't spend all your time trying to prove a point. Believe me. I know what that's like. It's not healthy."

"You think there's something wrong with me?"

"I didn't say that. I think you need to relax, to enjoy life."

"But I need to study."

"You need to live, to quit being so afraid of failure. We all fail sometimes in our lives." As I say those words, I feel as if I'm speaking as much to myself as to Danny.

"What have you ever failed at, Mr. C?" he asks skeptically.

"I've failed to be what my father wanted me to be. And he's never forgiven me for that." I say the words so quickly, so matter-of-factly, that it takes me a second to comprehend their significance. Rising, I turn away from Danny, feeling embarrassed and a little ashamed. "That's the first time I've admitted that to anyone."

"How can you be a failure, Mr. Collins?"

"I'm not," I respond, facing him again. "That's the whole point. And neither are you. Sometimes people who love us have unrealistic expectations. They see in us only what they want to see. We can't let their expectations run our lives. We're the ones who know us best; who know what we're capable of doing, of being. It's important we set our own goals and values, that we accept ourselves, regardless of what others think."

"But my father has no expectations for me. He doesn't think I'll amount to anything."

"I think he does. I think it's his way of coping with your learning disability. If he tells himself he has no expectations, then in his way of thinking, he can't be disappointed."

Danny nods his head, but uncertainty still clouds in his eyes.

"Just think about what I said, all right?"

"Okay, Mr. C."

"Good. Now, what about your mother? She's very worried not knowing where you are."

"Could you call her in the morning? Please. I don't want a hassle with her now."

I hear the desperation in his voice. I fear that if I push the issue too much, I'll lose him, lose the trust we have between us. Besides, what do I have to lose by waiting? It's nearly two in the morning, and I'm already out of a job.

"All right, Danny."

"You mind if I stay?"

I'm certain my concern shows on my face.

"I won't tell anyone, Mr. C. And I know you're not gay."

"It just might look bad, Danny."

"Okay. I'll go."

"Wait." *What does it matter now what anyone thinks?* "You're welcome to use the bed. I'll drive you to school in the morning."

"Where are you going to sleep, Mr. C? The chair?"

"I have a cot in the storage closet."

"I'll sleep on the cot."

"I don't mind, Danny."

"I don't mind either."

"Fine. I'll set up the cot."

"Do you have a match?" he asks hesitantly, taking a package of cigarettes out of his jacket pocket.

"You think smoking's a good idea?"

"I don't do it much."

"Look around. There may be a book of matches somewhere."

He stands, looks on top of the nightstand and then—before I can tell him to stop—he opens the nightstand drawer.

"There are no matches in there, Danny."

He stares into the open drawer a moment before he closes it and looks at me without expression.

"Why don't you check the kitchen while I set up the cot."

He nods and shuffles into the kitchen.

While he's there, I take Jack Stone's gun out of the nightstand drawer, holding it carefully with the barrel pointed down, and put it in my chest of drawers under some sweaters.

Later, when the lights are out and Danny lies on the cot, he says, "I'm the reason my parents got divorced, you know."

"That's not true."

"It is, too. I remember when I was young, before my parents found out I had a learning disability. They were really happy then. We all were happy. If it hadn't been for my problem, they wouldn't have argued all the time. They'd still be married now."

"Believe me, it wasn't your fault."

"I appreciate you saying that, Mr. Collins. But it doesn't change anything. My parents are still divorced. And I know why."

I lie still for a time, feeling beads of sweat forming between my back and the sheets, listening to the wail of a distant siren and the low hum of the fan as it pushes the warm air from one side of the room to the other.

"Since I was in junior high," Danny says, "my dream has been to be a success, not just athletically, but academically. I always wanted to go to the university where my father teaches and get into engineering. If I don't pass English, I'm finished."

"I know it's hard to believe there are teachers like Bruder still in the system, Danny. They're difficult to deal with. They've got tenure, and school boards are reluctant to confront them because of the union. But you know most teachers aren't like that."

Moonlight shining in the window casts enough of a glow that I can see the outline of Danny's body. He lies on his back, hands behind his head, looking at the ceiling. I have a sinking feeling that nothing I say matters.

"Maybe I should talk to Jack Stone," Danny says. "Try and convince him that you should read me Bruder's exam."

"We'd probably have more luck talking to your mother and having her call a few school board members."

"Leave my mother out of this. I want to do this on my own."

"I'll help you study. You'll pass."

"And if I don't?"

"It's not the end of the world."

"Maybe not for you. But it is for me."

I can't help but see the irony of the situation. Here I am trying to reassure Danny, telling him it isn't the end of the world if he loses his scholarship, when I feel exactly the same way about losing my teaching position.

I go into the bathroom and turn on the light. My neck is still sore. I swallow two aspirin from a bottle in the medicine cabinet and wash the pills down with a glass of water. Then I turn out the light and get back into bed.

I can't shake the guilt I have about not calling Danny's mother. I know she's concerned. Still, I empathize with Danny, especially with the feelings he has for his father. And yet, I know I haven't dealt with those feelings any better than he has. In fact, I haven't dealt with any real feelings since I went to see Laura's psychiatrist five years ago.

* * *

Dr. Peter Dressler's address was listed on his card. His office was located in York Plaza, the newest in a series of malls designed to cater to the charge card mentality in everyone. A half dozen little shops, with not-so-little prices, encircled a large pillared atrium. The sun's weak winter rays filtered through a vast skylight overhead. Water arched from a marble fountain. The elevators in the plaza had glass on one side, so as I rode one jammed with clones in Brooks Brothers suits up to the fifteenth floor, I could view the terra firma sinking away from me. Some engineer's idea of fun, no doubt.

As I opened the door and entered Dr. Dressler's waiting room, a middle-aged blonde receptionist greeted me with a smile and a warm, "Hello."

"I'm Michael Collins. I have an appointment to see Dr. Dressler."

"Please have a seat, Mr. Collins. I'll let the doctor know you're here."

I sat down on the leather couch. New Age music played in the background. I paged through a copy of *Time* for about ten minutes before the receptionist said, "Dr. Dressler will see you now."

The doctor's office was small, with thick beige carpeting and bookshelves that lined two walls.

"How do you do, Mr. Collins?" Dr. Dressler smiled and came around his desk and shook my hand.

He was younger than I expected, perhaps in his late thirties. He was about my height and weight and had dark, curly hair, a broad forehead, and flared nostrils. He wore a navy blue turtleneck sweater and a pair of pleated gray pants and black loafers.

"Would you like coffee, tea, or water?"

"No, thanks."

"Please sit down."

I sat down in a chair opposite the desk. Though the room was cool, sweat dampened the back of my shirt.

"Ever been to a psychiatrist before?"

"No, I haven't."

"It can be intimidating for some people."

"Doesn't bother me," I lied. "Besides, I'm here to talk about Laura."

"You're aware I can't discuss specifics."

"I thought you might say that, Doctor. But I need some help in understanding what's happening to her. What's happening to us."

The leather chair behind his desk let out a sigh as he settled himself. "You're in love with Laura?"

"Very much."

"I can understand your concern." He poured himself a cup of tea from the teapot on his desk and took a sip. Music played softly in the quiet of the room. "Does Laura know you're here?"

"No. I found your card next to her purse. I think she considered calling you, but she's afraid."

"Afraid of what?"

"Of what you'll find."

He looked at the teacup in his hands a moment before his gaze returned to me. "Are you afraid?"

"Yes. But not of what you'll find. I'm more afraid of what'll happen if she doesn't get some help. And soon."

He sipped more tea. "How much do you know about Laura's background?"

His calm demeanor began to annoy me. "I know her mother is institutionalized. I know Laura's had severe mood swings lately. I know you're her psychiatrist. I know she's frightened, and so am I. Outside of that, not much, Doctor."

He sat forward and placed the cup gently in a saucer and set it on the desk. "Laura's been having severe mood swings?" he said with obvious concern in his voice.

"Yes," I replied, pleased that I've finally gotten his attention.

"Explain."

I told him about Laura's explosive outburst the night she accused me of not wanting her to finish her Ph.D. I told him about her going for days without sleep before exhaustion overtook her and she collapsed, often in a state of depression. And I told him about the night with Cameron and Monica Ford when she came downstairs naked.

"Have you spoken with Laura about her behavior?"

I could see Laura in my mind's eye, see her standing naked and helpless, feel the chill that ran through me as the image dissolved, and I saw her again in the arms of Cameron Ford.

"Yes," I said.

"How did she react?"

"I told you. She's frightened. Frightened that she'll end up in an institution like her mother. That's why I need your help, Doctor."

He sat perfectly still, hardly seeming to breathe. "There's something else," he said at last.

"What do you mean?"

"Why don't you tell me?"

Suddenly I felt trapped in the small room. I couldn't tell him about Cameron Ford any more than I could tell Laura that I knew about her affair with him. I was too afraid of losing her, and so I'd made up excuses for her and lies for myself. All the scenarios I'd pictured in my mind ran together like colors in a wash. Having imagined an ending in which she'd beg forgiveness, in which she'd accept blame, I was left with a feeling of incompleteness. All I knew was that something was terribly wrong with her, and whatever it was, it was destroying both of us.

"Look, Dr. Dressler, I came here to talk about Laura, not about me."

"You don't want to talk about your anger."

"I already told you what I'm upset about."

"All right," he responded, unperturbed. He sat back, rested an elbow on the arm of his chair, and placed an index finger on his lips, contemplating.

I could almost hear the inner workings of his mind. "You know, this reminds me of a first date."

"It does?"

"Whenever the conversation lags, I feel like I have to say something."

He smiled. "I'm sorry if my reticence makes you nervous."

"But not sorry enough that you're going to tell me much."

"You seem to know quite a bit. Why don't you tell me what else you know and we'll proceed from there?"

"Okay. Laura told me she came to see you about a year and a half ago."

He nodded. "I'd done some consulting work at the university, primarily with students, so we had a passing acquaintance."

"That would be just before we met." My mind flashed back to the first time I saw Laura standing in the airplane aisle, telling me her headphones didn't work. "Until recently, Laura never talked to me about her family. I thought her mother had died of cancer."

"Do you know anything about her father?"

"Only that he was a missionary in the Far East. Laura said he died at a relatively young age."

"Yes, I believe he was in his late forties. Laura's mother was nearly forty when Laura was born."

"When Laura talked about her father, I got the feeling that she loved him very much."

Dressler sat silently in his chair, looking at me.

I continued. "Her mother became ill right after they returned to the States. The doctors were able to control her illness with drugs for a time, but her mother gradually became worse. Treatment resistant, Laura called it. Eventually her mother had to be institutionalized at the state hospital in St. Clair."

"It happens in a small number of cases." Dressler looked at me stoically and sipped more tea.

I decided it was my turn to ask some questions. "So, tell me, Dr. Dressler, what causes bipolar disorder?"

"The cause is not entirely known. Genetic, neurochemical, and environmental factors probably play a role in its onset and progression. The current thinking is that it's predominantly a biological disorder that occurs in a specific part of the brain due to a malfunction of the neurotransmitters, or chemical messengers. As a biological disorder, it may lie dormant and be activated spontaneously, or stressors in life like the loss of a loved one might trigger it."

"What's affecting Laura? What makes her act like she does?"

"We've come a long way in the last ten years in understanding affective disorders and in improving treatment, Mr. Collins," he replied, ignoring my question. "That's what you should concentrate on."

"I need to know more about Laura's condition," I persisted. "So I can help her."

This time he seemed to consider the question. "A tendency toward bipolar disorder does run in some families."

"What can I do?"

"You can encourage Laura to come in for treatment."

"Encourage? That's all?"

He nodded. "If Laura doesn't want to come in, there's nothing you can do."

Chapter 15

Kate Fleming's casket, laced with brightly colored flowers, sits on a bier at her gravesite, surrounded by mourners dressed in black. Headstones stretch out around me in all directions. The air is heavy with the fragrance of funeral flowers, the odors of lilies, roses and carnations. Birds chirp. A stiff breeze blows.

I stand between Mac Tyler and Beth Stanton at one end of the open grave atop a knoll, feeling the press of the crowd around me, looking down at the darkness and the damp musty dirt of the open hole. Jack Stone stands at the opposite end.

I can't look at him, can't bring myself to go over to him and say . . . what? What can I say? *Sorry I slept with your wife, old boy, but it's over now, no reason we still can't be friends. After all, we'll be working together next fall.* Sure we will.

I wonder what Jack is thinking. I've wondered ever since this morning when I watched him striding up the steps of the cathedral. I made certain that I gave him plenty of time to get seated before I got out of my car and entered the church. Once inside, I let my eyes adjust to the dim light, scanning the crowd until I found Jack. I took a seat in a pew far enough behind him to feel safe, but not far enough behind that I would lose sight of him.

Now, as I stand by Kate Fleming's grave, I imagine Jack coming at me again with his thick fingers outstretched. My neck begins hurting all over again as I feel the vise-like grip of his hands around my throat and hear Nicole scream.

Nicole.

The thought hits me with the force of a punch. I've been so focused, so intent on Jack, that I haven't even thought about

Nicole. *Why isn't she here? Has something happened to her?* I have to suppress the frightening thought that flashes in my mind.

"We never had any children," John Fleming says to the throng gathered around the gravesite. As he speaks, the sun peeks out from behind gray stratus clouds as if trying to get a better look. "Kate dedicated herself to the students at Wilson," he continues. "Those were her children."

John Fleming has suffered a terrible loss. I've lost my job, my relationship with my father—and Laura. Loss. Life is really all about loss. Friends move away. Lovers part. Family members die. Everyone is constantly losing someone or something. Knowing that hardly makes me feel any better.

The priest offers his closing remarks and then leads John Fleming and a procession of relatives and close friends away from the gravesite and down the hill toward the cars that are lined along the drive.

"Beth and I are going to get a drink," Mac says to me. "You want to come and toast one for Kate?"

I consider saying yes. Leaving with Mac and Beth would be the safest course of action, but something urges me to stay. I shake my head. "I think I'll wait around for a while."

Mac nods.

I look at Beth. Her eyes are red from crying. Mac puts his big arm around her shoulder and leads her away.

A small group lingers by Kate's casket. I recognize a few of my students, but Danny O'Brien isn't one of them.

I recall the alarm jarring me awake this morning and how, after shutting it off, I lay still for a moment, feeling logy and focusing my eyes. I remember rolling over, looking at the empty cot next to the bed, and feeling my heartbeat increase, thinking as I sit up, *Maybe he's in the bathroom?* Then when I called, "Danny," and there was no answer, I realized that he was gone.

I telephoned his mother and asked if she had heard anything from him. When she said, "No," I left it at that. Although

I knew where he had been last night, I didn't know where he was at that moment, so as far as we both were concerned, Danny was missing.

Slowly, those students who have lingered by Kate's casket move off, one by one, in pairs and in groups, until there are only two of us left. Through sheer force of will I'm able to raise my head and look at Jack Stone standing at the opposite end of the grave. I no longer hear the birds or the wind, only the sound of my heart thudding in my chest and pounding in my ears. My mouth is dry, and I fight the sudden urge to leap into the open grave. I picture Jack with a shovel, throwing dirt on me as I lie at the bottom.

I stare at Jack Stone, not speaking or moving, waiting for something, anything to happen, and then it occurs to me that maybe Jack wants it this way. Maybe he wants me to wait and wonder, never knowing what he has in mind for me. Maybe this is his way of extracting revenge. And though I know I'm guilty as charged, know that I should willingly accept punishment, a part of me rebels at this notion of revenge.

"It's finished, Jack," I say, in a voice that sounds hollow and weaker than I would have liked. "All finished."

His eyes lock on mine, as if in silent combat. "No," he replies flatly. "It's not finished. Not yet." He turns and walks down the hill to his parked pickup.

* * *

"Hello?" Nicole answers.

I sped away from the gravesite in a state of panic, all the while imagining Nicole a victim in a set of tragic circumstances. Shot. Hanged. Stabbed. Drowned. Now that I hear her voice, know that she's safe, I feel like a fool. I think momentarily of breaking off the connection.

"Michael? Are you okay?"

"I'm fine. And you?"

"Worried," she says. "I'm worried about Jack. I haven't heard from him."

"I saw him at Kate Fleming's funeral this morning."

"Was he all right? How did he look?"

It occurs to me now that Jack looked menacing, that he always looks menacing. "He looked . . . fine."

"I'm sorry I didn't attend, Michael. But I just couldn't go. Not after what happened last night. Not after that."

"I understand."

"Did Jack say anything to you?"

I wonder if I should tell her what Jack said, what he threatened, then think better of it. *What good will it do to panic her?*

"No," I reply. "He never said a word to me."

"Oh."

"I wonder what he's up to?" I say, thinking out loud.

"Maybe he's not up to anything, Michael. Maybe he's just hurt and needs some time to sort things out." Her tone is less convincing than her words.

"Maybe."

There's a long pause.

"Was there something else, Michael?"

"Something else?"

"Another reason why you called?"

"I guess I was worried about you."

"Thank you for still caring. That means a lot."

I don't know how to respond, and so I say nothing.

"Are you frightened, Michael?"

"I'm not sure what I am. Are you?"

"Yes," she says. "Jack has a temper."

"I'm aware of that."

"I've never seen him that angry. Never. How's your neck?"

"Sore."

"I'm sorry it had to happen, Michael."

"It didn't have to happen."

"Do you think so?"

"I do."

"I'm inclined to believe that everything happens for a purpose," she says.

"Really."

"Yes."

"Everything?"

"Yes. Everything."

"Even your son's death?"

She doesn't respond right away. I start to apologize for bringing up her son's death when she says, "Yes. Even that."

There's another lengthy pause.

Finally I say, "Well, good-bye, Mrs. Stone."

"Good-bye, Michael."

I feel an odd sense of loss as I break off the call, though unlike the feeling I experienced at Kate Fleming's funeral this morning, I have no idea now what it is that I've lost. I remember feeling the same way when I broke up with Pam. Two different relationships, neither one involving love, and yet I feel as if I've lost a part of myself. Maybe that's it. You can't help but give something of yourself when you're in a relationship. When it's over, no one is exactly the same as they were before. And if you give a part of yourself in every failed relationship, I wonder how long it takes before you have nothing left to give?

I look at my watch. 5:00 p.m. In two hours I'm supposed to have dinner at my parents' house. I have no desire to attend a party in my honor, a party celebrating a job I no longer have, but that's only part of it. I have no desire to attend a birthday party for my father either. Then again, it might take my mind off tomorrow, when I have to face Jack Stone again.

Back in my apartment, I shave and take a long cooling shower, forcing myself to concentrate on the shower itself rather than on what the future might hold. Afterwards, I put on a pair of cotton shorts, a polo shirt, and running shoes. Then I call Danny O'Brien's house. No answer. *Now what?* I decide to take my mother's advice and come early.

On the way, I stop at a drugstore to buy a birthday card for my father. As I read through the verses, trying to select an appropriate card, I realize that they all imply a wonderful relationship between father and son, a relationship like we used to have before I quit baseball.

I remember the last time that I pitched five years ago. The Mets had taken me to spring training with them based on my outstanding season the previous year, but my mind wasn't on baseball. It was on Laura. I had a couple of rough outings, so the Mets sent me to their minor league camp. Just before the team broke training camp and headed for New York, Johnny Desmond called me into his office.

* * *

"They want you," he said.

Still in his uniform with the blue piping down the pants legs, Johnny pushed his cap back on his head and put his feet up on the corner of his desk. His spikes were off and the stirrups on his blue socks hung loose, revealing the soiled bottoms of his white sanitary hose. Paunchy now, his skin tanned and weathered from the sun, he drank from a bottle of Budweiser. Behind him in the center of the concrete wall was a faded framed picture of the world champion '69 Mets.

He belched and said, "McNeil's hurt his arm, and they need a lefty in the rotation to start the season. You haven't pitched that well this spring, but you've got talent, kid. I saw plenty of it last summer."

Johnny Desmond was never a great player, bouncing around with six different clubs in his seven years in the majors, mostly as a utility infielder, but he was a great manager.

"You pitch in New York like you did for me last year, Collins, you'll go a long way. Good lefties are hard to find."

"Thanks for everything, Coach."

"You don't seem too excited."

I shrugged.

He gave me a half-smile. "I've been around this game a long time. I know when someone's head isn't right. Whatever's troubling you, kid, don't let it ruin your career. You'll be in New York by morning."

Or home, I thought. I nodded and headed for the door.

"It's what you've been training for your whole life, kid. The big show. This is it."

"Yes," I said, suddenly knowing what I'd do. "It is."

* * *

I place a check for twenty bucks in a plain card that just reads, HAPPY BIRTHDAY, DAD, and put the card inside an envelope. I know that it won't matter what I bring him now. I wonder for a moment if Danny O'Brien has the same thoughts about his father.

My mother is in the kitchen, putting the finishing touches on a bowl of potato salad, when I walk in the back door. The aroma of freshly baked chocolate cake fills the kitchen.

"You're early!" she says in surprise and gives me a hug. "Rick and Joan aren't even here yet." Holding me at arm's length, she says suddenly, "Michael. What on earth did you do to your neck?"

I'm prepared for this. "Wrestling."

"Wrestling?"

I sense her skepticism. "With Mac. We were just horsing around. It got a little out of hand."

"Oh," she says, continuing to stare at my neck.

"Sure smells great in here, Mom."

She nods.

"Real great."

She nods again.

She knows. Like she knows everything else.

She looked over my shoulder. "You didn't bring Pam?"

Great. "I'm not seeing Pam anymore."

She gazes into my eyes a moment as if seeking an explanation.

"What's for dinner?" I ask.

"Hamburgers. Your father's out back getting the charcoal started."

"He must be in the garage. I didn't see him when I drove up." I walk over to the counter, run a forefinger around the edge of a mixing bowl, and lick the chocolate off my finger. As I turn around, I realize that my mother is still staring at me.

"It's Laura, isn't it?" she says at last.

I accidentally bite my finger. "What makes you say that?"

"Because you're still in love with her. You've always been in love with her."

"You're really serious, aren't you?" I say with a little laugh.

"I've never asked what happened between you two," she says. "And I'm not asking now."

I know what I should say, but the words catch in my throat. I look away and shrug my shoulders like some recalcitrant teenager.

My mother wipes her hands on the apron tied around her waist and begins sprinkling paprika on top of the potato salad. "Why don't you bring your father a beer?"

"Okay," I say, thankful that she has let me off the hook about Laura. I'm not sure why I can't tell her. I only know that I have to tell someone—and soon.

I hand her the birthday card I bought for my father, take two cans of Miller out of the refrigerator, and open the back door. A wave of heat hits me, as if I've just opened an oven.

"Talk to him, Michael," she says. "Please talk to your father."

I nod and walk out into the yard, closing the back door behind me. My father is pouring charcoal fluid on the coals in the grill. "Happy birthday, Dad."

"What's happy about another birthday?"

"You can retire soon. Enjoy life."

"Some of us enjoy working," he says, making a small pile out of the coals.

I'm uncertain if his remark is meant for me or if I'm being overly sensitive, but rather than ruin the evening, I hold out a can of Miller and say, "Have a beer."

"In a minute." Sweat rings the underarms of his khaki shirt.

I bought him shorts for his birthday once, but he refused to wear them. "Tough starting the coals with all this humidity, huh?" I say, trying to make conversation.

"I'll get 'em lit."

"You should use those coals that start without fluid. Or buy yourself a gas grill."

"There's nothing wrong with coals. I've used the same brand for years." He lights a match and throws it in the grill, setting the coals on fire. "I'll take that beer now," he says with a triumphant smile.

I pass him a can and step back from the heat of the flames. For an instant I wish the coals hadn't lit. Then I feel angry with myself for having had such a petty thought.

We stand there, the two of us, watching the flames and drinking beer, until finally I say, "Tornado weather," falling back on a familiar topic of conversation.

"Not a cloud in the sky," he replies, looking up. Sweat beads on his forehead.

Condensation trickles down the sides of his beer can. The flames recede.

I drink some more beer and look at the small green apples that have replaced the white flowers of spring on the two apple trees in the yard. A tall oak shades half the yard, a lower branch scarred where a rope and tire once hung.

"So you're going to be a full-time teacher," he says, not looking at me but in the general direction of the neighbor's yard.

"Possibly," I reply, hoping to avoid any further discussion.

Now he looks directly at me. "Your mother said it was all set. You'd been offered a job."

"I was."

"Don't tell me after all this time you're not going to take it."

"Of course I'll take it," I say, trying to keep my voice from rising.

"Well, then, what's the problem?"

"No problem."

"You sounded like there was a problem."

"I said there wasn't."

"Christ almighty," he says. "All this time looking for a job that pays pauper's wages and now you don't know if you'll even accept it when it's finally offered to you."

"I didn't say that. You're not listening. You never listen to me anymore."

"Oh, we're on that again, huh?" He puts down his beer can, picks up the bottle of charcoal fluid on the ground, and douses the now flameless coals.

"Look, Dad. It's your birthday. Let's not get into it."

"Get into what?" he says, flipping a lighted match on the coals. They burst into flame again.

"You know."

He glares at me. "You mean how you've been shuffling from job to job? How you've spent your last dollar on graduate school that was supposed to get you a good job? How your brother has been working his fanny off helping me keep the family business afloat?"

"Don't give me that garbage about the family business, Dad. You never cared if I came into the business. That's got nothing to do with what's eating you."

"Oh. So something's supposed to be eating me."

"We both know what it is."

"Now you're some kind of shrink?"

"We've got to talk about this, Dad. Get it straightened out."

"We've got nothing to talk about."

"That's not true."

"Don't tell me what's true and what isn't. You're the one who messed up your life, the one who threw away a one in a million chance to really make something of yourself, to really be somebody. A chance I never had."

"So that's what you think?"

"It's not what I think," he says, the veins bulging in his thick neck. "It's what I know."

"Aw, fuck it. What's the use?" I toss the half-empty can of beer across the yard and walk toward my car parked in the driveway, head down, anger churning like undigested food in my stomach.

"Is that what you learned from all that education?" he calls after me. "How to swear?"

"That I learned from you!" I yell back.

"Michael!"

I glance up. My mother is standing on the back step, looking at me as if suddenly I'm a stranger she doesn't know. It's that look that tugs at my heart, which holds on and won't let go as I get in my car and drive away.

Chapter 16

The wave of anger recedes slowly, leaving tightness in my chest. Part of me feels guilty about what has happened. I know there's nothing worse than quitting in my father's eyes. The word is an expletive. It's a message Rick and I heard from the time we were old enough to pick up our first baseball.

* * *

The summer my brother, Rick, was twelve and I was ten, we both played Little League baseball on the same team. My father was the manager.

In late July, as we were battling for the championship and the right to represent the league in the state tournament, my father and Rick got into an argument in the dugout between innings.

"Rick, how many times have I told you?" my father said. "You can't see the ball clearly with your mask on when there's a play at the plate."

"I see fine. The throw was up the line. I couldn't make the tag."

"The throw was right to you. If you can't do what I tell you, I'll put somebody behind the plate who can."

Three innings later, on another close play at the plate, with the game on the line, a relay throw took a wicked bounce between the pitcher's mound and home. Rick, who had taken off his mask, was struck in the forehead and knocked unconscious.

The coaches and players from both teams gathered in a hushed circle around Rick. I walked over and picked up the catcher's mask he'd tossed before being struck with the baseball. I held it so tightly that my hand ached.

"He isn't waking up, Carl," the home plate umpire said. "You'd better get him to the hospital."

My parents rode in the ambulance with Rick while a coach drove me to Hennepin General. When I got to the emergency room, Rick still had not regained consciousness.

"What if he doesn't wake up?" I said to my mother.

"He will. I know he will."

"What are you doing with that?" my father said.

I looked down at the fielder's glove in my left hand and the catcher's mask I held in my right. "I picked it up at the field. I didn't remember I had it."

"You didn't remember?"

"No."

He looked at me for a time but said nothing.

A young doctor came out to the hallway where we were seated and said, "We'd like to do a brain scan."

My mother looked over at my father and then at me. I could see the fear in her eyes.

"Whatever you need to do," my father said. "Do it."

The doctor nodded and went away.

An hour later he returned and told us that the brain scan showed no bleeding and no apparent damage. He was at a loss to explain why Rick had not regained consciousness. He said they were moving him to a room on the second floor. There was nothing we could do now but wait.

I sat on a chair between my parents in the second-floor lounge near Rick's room. Sand shifted inside my rubber-cleated shoes, and I shivered with a sudden chill as my sweat evaporated in the air-conditioned hospital.

"I'm going to get some coffee, Carl," my mother said. "Do you want some?"

He shook his head.

"Do you want a Coke, Michael?"

"Okay."

"Want to come with me?"

"I'll wait here."

She stood up, gave me a reassuring smile, and walked down the hallway and around a corner.

"Long day, huh?" my father said.

"Yeah."

"Long day for all of us." He stood up, lit a cigarette and inhaled deeply. He paced in front of me and smoked. After a time, he stopped pacing and looked at me. I knew he wanted to say something.

"I always taught you boys that there's a right way and a wrong way to do something, no in-between. Isn't that so?"

I nodded.

"And things have worked out pretty well, haven't they?"

"Sure, Dad."

He crushed out his cigarette in a canister ashtray and sat down next to me again.

"Where the hell's your mother? Something could happen, and she wouldn't know. That isn't right." He coughed twice, rubbed his pants legs, and let out a long sigh.

"She just went to get some coffee," I said.

"I know that. Don't you think I know that?"

I looked away from him and fumbled with the straps on the catcher's mask in my lap. The bars and padding along the top and bottom of the mask were covered with dust, and one of the rivets that held the strap was loose.

We sat quietly for a few minutes until my father said, "Maybe I should've let it go. Maybe I should've just let it go." He got up again and walked over to a window and looked out.

"Dad?" I said.

"What?"

"Were you ever in a hospital?"

"Sure."

"When?"

"When I was a kid. I had my tonsils out."

"Did it hurt?"

"Some."

"Weren't you in a hospital when you were wounded in Vietnam?"

He turned and looked at me. "Yes," he said.

"How long?"

"Long enough."

"Did you almost lose your arm?"

"No. It wasn't that serious."

"But you got to come home."

"Yes, I did. I was lucky."

"But you couldn't pitch anymore. You couldn't play baseball."

"No, I couldn't."

"What if Rick can't play baseball anymore?"

"Your brother's going to be fine. He's got a concussion. Happens to kids every day."

"But what if he couldn't play? What if I couldn't play? What then?"

"What are you saying? You don't want to play baseball anymore? You want to quit?"

"No," I said. "I love baseball, and Rick does, too. I was just wondering what would happen if we couldn't play anymore."

"Nothing would happen," he said.

"What would we do?"

"We'd do what most people do."

"What's that?"

"Nothing. That's what most people do. Nothing."

"I was just wondering."

"Well, don't wonder. And don't say it. Don't even think about quitting. You don't ever want to be known as a quitter."

I was thirteen years old before I understood why my father placed so much importance on not quitting. That was the year a friend of his came to visit. His name was Sandy Phillips, and he had served with my father during the war. Though I met Sandy Phillips only that one time, he helped me understand my father more than anyone ever had or ever would.

* * *

My father was away hauling a load of freight to Oregon when Sandy Phillips showed up at our door early one evening in late August, as summer entered its final innings.

My mother had heard my father speak of Sandy, and she recognized his face from photos my father kept in a scrapbook of the Vietnam War. On his way to Ohio for a wedding, Sandy had decided he would detour north to Minnesota and visit my father, whom he hadn't seen in nearly twenty years. My mother invited him in for dinner and, despite his protestations, insisted that he use the hide-a-bed in the recreation room downstairs instead of paying for a motel room.

Sandy stood about five feet eight inches and combed his thinning hair, which was the color of a shiny new baseball, straight back. His face was an oval. Pockmarked and light complected, it appeared permanently sunburned. His eyes were such a light blue as to render them nearly translucent.

At dinner Sandy asked Rick and me about baseball and what positions we played. He drank glasses of vodka and grapefruit juice and told us his favorite team was the Cleveland Indians even though they hadn't had a great club since 1954.

"They won one hundred and eleven games and the pennant that year," Sandy said. "Bob Lemon and Early Wynn won twenty-three games apiece. Mike Garcia won nineteen. They had Bob Feller, Al Rosen, Larry Doby and Bobby Avila. Hell of a club. And the Giants swept them four straight in the World

Series?" He shook his head in disbelief and drank from his glass of vodka and grapefruit juice.

I went with Rick and Sandy to the field across the street for a game of work-up while my mother cleared the supper dishes. Sandy wasn't very coordinated, but what he lacked in ability he made up for in enthusiasm. We played for an hour before we sat under a maple tree and took a break. Sandy offered us each a Tootsie Roll.

"Did you know my dad before the war?" Rick asked.

"Met him in basic training in California. We were both eighteen. I tried to talk him into starting a charter fishing service on the coast after our hitch was up, if your dad didn't make it in pro ball. That was his first love. But he probably told you all his war stories."

"He never told us anything," I said.

"Is that right?"

We sat under the maple tree, ate our Tootsie Rolls, and watched the sun fade like a flare on the horizon.

"What was it like there?" I asked. "In Vietnam."

"Hot, humid, and wet. I'm still dealing with jungle rot."

"What's that?" Rick asked.

"Athlete's foot. Most everyone got it from walking in rice paddies and rain-soaked jungles. When I got home, I stayed in northern California. I never want to live in hot, humid weather again."

"Were you ever wounded?" I asked.

"Sure was. And if it weren't for your dad, I wouldn't be here today. He saved my life."

"Really?" Rick said.

"You better believe it."

I'd always respected my father, and when it came to discipline, I suppose I feared him. But I'd never thought of him as a hero, slaying dragons or saving men.

"How?" Rick said. "How did he save your life?"

"We'd been in 'Nam six months," Sandy began. "We were west of Da Nang en route to assist another unit that was engaged with the enemy. We came under intense enemy fire, and the lead man was killed instantly."

"Were you scared?" I asked.

"Never been more scared in my life," Sandy said. "But you didn't have much time to think about it. The fear comes afterward, after the shooting is over."

"What happened then?" Rick asked.

"Your dad moved to the head of the column, and together we knocked out two enemy bunkers."

"Just the two of you?" I said.

"Well, everyone was shooting. But your dad and I kept moving forward. He spotted a Viet Cong sniper and killed him. He led repeated assaults against the enemy positions, killing several more Viet Cong. We were moving to attack two additional enemy bunkers and were drawing intense enemy fire when we were both blown off our feet by an enemy grenade."

"Is that when my dad nearly lost his arm?" I asked.

Sandy nodded.

"What about you?"

"I had a head wound and shrapnel in my legs. Your dad carried me to safety, replenished his ammunition, and took out the other bunker. He kept fighting till we were ordered to withdraw, dragging two more men to safety under heavy fire. The Army awarded him the Medal of Honor."

Rick had been tossing the baseball in his glove while he listened to Sandy recount the story, but now he sat as still as the humid air around us and looked at me. We were still in our teens, but we knew what the medal represented.

"Why didn't Dad ever say anything about it?" Rick asked.

Sandy took out a fresh handful of Tootsie Rolls and gave us a couple each. He unwrapped one, put it in his mouth, and leaned his back against the trunk of the maple tree.

In the distance I could hear the hum of a lawn mower and smell the sweet scent of freshly cut grass.

"Most men choose not to talk about their war experiences, boys."

"Why?" I asked.

"I hope you two never have to go to war. But if you do, you'll understand."

"How come you weren't killed?" Rick asked.

"I still ask myself that question sometimes." He paused a moment and gave us a quick smile. "I sure figured I was a goner. But your dad got me out of there. Lucky for me he did. Seems a bullet went through my helmet at an angle and spun around my head between the steel pot and the liner. Tore them both up and ripped open the right side of my skull. It felt like someone hit me with a baseball bat. I was afraid to touch my head, not knowing how much of it was left. To be honest, I didn't want to know. Helicopters airlifted us out, and a day later your dad and I were in Japan. A month after that we were stateside. We lost a lot of good men that day. Brave men. It never mattered much to me what happened afterwards. But your dad was pretty upset when we quit the war. All those who lost their lives died for nothing." He shook his head and ate another Tootsie Roll.

Dusk had settled, and squadrons of mosquitoes began using us for target practice. We gathered up our gear and walked silently across the field and back home.

The next morning Sandy Phillips left after a breakfast of vodka and grapefruit juice. I never saw him again, but my father would get a letter from him now and then. Sandy worked as a tree trimmer in the redwood forests of northern California and later ran a charter fishing service out of San Francisco Bay. Sandy had three ex-wives and no children. When he died of lung cancer, my father didn't go to his funeral.

* * *

My father looked out the hospital window near the wooden bench.

"Hey, Dad?" I said.

"What?"

"We didn't make the playoffs, did we?"

"No," he said. "We didn't make the playoffs. First year since I started coaching you boys that we didn't make some kind of playoff or state tournament."

"What are we going to do for the rest of the summer? I mean, when Rick gets better."

"What do you want to do?" he asked.

"Well, we could go fishing."

"Fishing? Since when did you start fishing?"

"I haven't. Ever."

He chuckled. "Not much action, son. Believe me."

"But I'd like to try."

"You'd like to try?"

"Yes," I said.

"Why?"

"I don't know."

"You don't know why you'd like to try something?"

I shrugged. "It's different."

"I think I've still got a tackle box in the garage."

"Really?" I said.

"Haven't used it in years."

"Could we?"

"You don't know anything about fishing."

"So? You could teach me."

"You'd be bored to death."

"Maybe I wouldn't."

"Trust me, son. I know what I'm talking about."

"Oh," I said.

I looked down the hallway and wondered what was taking my mother so long.

"How's your glove?" he said.

"My glove?"

"Do you need a new one?"

"My glove's fine," I said, and as if to demonstrate, I pounded the pocket with my fist.

"Good. Always pays to have the best equipment."

"What about a trip?" I asked. "Mom said she'd like to visit her sister in Phoenix. That would be fun."

"Summer is a peak time for the business," he said. "You know that."

"You take time off to coach."

"Coaching's different."

"I could come help you at the warehouse," I said.

"You're too young. Besides, you could hurt your arm like I hurt mine. You wouldn't want to do that, would you?"

"No," I said. "I wouldn't want to do that."

My mother came back with a cup of coffee and a Coke.

I drank the Coke and unwrapped two fresh pieces of Double Bubble gum that I had in the back pocket of my uniform and put them in my mouth between my tongue and cheek, pretending it was a wad of tobacco.

An hour passed before a nurse and a doctor went into Rick's room.

"What's wrong?" my mother said, standing.

"Nothing's wrong, Rose," my father said. "Nothing's wrong. They have to check on him periodically. That's all."

A lump formed like a bubble in my throat.

The doctor came out of Rick's room and walked over to us.

"Your son's awake," he said. "I think he'll be fine, but we want to keep him overnight. Just to make certain."

My mother opened her purse, took out a Kleenex, and dabbed her eyes.

"Can we see him now?" my father said, putting an arm around her shoulder.

"Of course," the doctor said.

We went into Rick's room. My mother brushed Rick's blond hair off his forehead, leaned over, and kissed him.

"I'm okay, Mom," he said. "You can stop crying."

She pulled a chair up right next to the bed and held Rick's hand and continued looking at him, like he might lapse into a coma if she took her eyes off him.

"You all right, Rick?" my father said.

"I've got a major league headache."

I walked over beside the bed. "Lucky you got hit in the head. Otherwise you might've really gotten hurt."

"Real funny, buddy," Rick said. He pointed to the catcher's mask in my hand. "That from the scene of the crime?"

"What do you mean?" my father said.

"Nothing," Rick said.

"I suppose you think I was wrong to tell you to take off your mask so you could see," my father said. "That it's my fault you're lying here in the hospital with a concussion."

"No," Rick said. "I didn't say that."

"But that's what you meant."

"Carl," my mother said. "Not now."

My father reached out and took the catcher's mask out of my hand and put it on. He placed his hands on his hips and looked at the three of us.

"I can't see a thing," he said. "Not a damn thing."

Chapter 17

I drive in the general direction of my apartment, not wanting to go home but not really knowing where else to go. The temperature hovers around ninety. My stomach growls with hunger, though I don't feel much like eating.

I locate Danny O'Brien's address on my cell phone using Google. I haven't been able to make it right with my father. Maybe I can still help Danny make it right with his.

Karen O'Brien lives in small, two-story stucco about a mile from Wilson High School. Two large spruce trees, one on each side of the walk, shade the front of the house. The yard is small, the dark blue shutters chipped and peeled, the green grass patchy and long and in need of a trim.

I ring the doorbell. An air-conditioner in one of the windows purrs like a large slumbering cat. Danny's mother opens the front door after the second ring.

"Yes?" she says, and then, apparently recognizing me from parent conferences, she adds, "Oh, hello."

"Hi. Is Danny home?"

"No. He was here early this morning, but he left again. He was very upset. I don't know where he's gone." Her eyes film, and she takes a deep breath, managing to hold back the tears.

An awkward silence ensues. I can see that Danny takes after her, with her strawberry blonde hair, freckles, and slenderness.

"Why didn't you call me last night when Danny came to see you?" she says at last. "Why?"

"I was afraid he'd run. I didn't want to jeopardize the trust we had between us." Her disdainful expression tells me that no matter what I say, it isn't going to make any difference. "I thought I was doing the right thing. I'm sorry."

Her body stiffens. "You should be sorry," she says and slams the door in my face.

I stand on the front steps of the O'Brien house, sweating in the heat, wondering what else I could have said, what would have made a difference. I knock on the door again, intending to ask her where her husband lives. Maybe if I explain the situation to him, he'll be able to work things out with Danny. I knock a few more times before I realize she isn't going to answer.

I drive around awhile, stopping at some of the teen hangouts in town, hoping to find Danny O'Brien. I spot his girlfriend, Ann Robbins, at a pizza place, but she says she hasn't seen Danny. Nearing my apartment, I stop at a liquor store and pick up a six-pack of Coors and take it home with me.

I put the oscillating fan on the kitchen counter and sit down at the table and pour the beer into a glass mug. I drink slowly, savoring the ice-cold flavor.

After I open my third can of beer, I take the wrinkled photograph I have of Laura out of my wallet and look at it. I recall being jarred awake one night a few months ago. I was dreaming about her, and in the dream, I couldn't see her face, couldn't remember what she looked like. It was the first time I had ever been unable to remember.

As I stare at the photograph now, pain and sadness move across my heart like a shadow. I recall the exact moment that I lost her, the exact moment that I betrayed the beautiful, trusting face in the picture.

* * *

"Hi, Michael," Laura said. "It's me."

"Do you know it's four o'clock in the morning?"

"Really? I hadn't noticed. I'm not very tired. Why don't you come over, Michael? We can watch the sunrise together. It will be absolutely beautiful."

"You need sleep, Laura. We both do."

"Nonsense. Just think of how many hours a person wastes in bed . . . I don't mean in bed . . . I don't consider that a waste of time . . . when we're in bed together." She laughed. "What I mean is, when we're in bed sleeping . . . sleep perchance to dream . . . Shakespeare! Sleep perchance to dream . . . and if you can't sleep or dream . . . use whipped cream." She laughed again.

"Are you all right?"

"Of course . . . I'm absolutely wonderful . . . never felt better . . . I think I'll write a letter."

"I'm coming over."

"Come on over, red rover . . . We'll take a walk . . . And talk . . . Don't balk, Michael . . . Pitchers aren't supposed to balk." She was into a laughing jag now, a deep, heaving fit of laughter.

The first thing I saw when I walked into her living room were hats and hat boxes stacked on the floor and the furniture; hats of different colors and shapes, hundreds of dollars' worth of hats. In all our time together, I had never known Laura to wear a hat. The month before it had been shoes. Six hundred dollars' worth of shoes, charged on her credit cards. It had taken me two days to return them all and get her money back.

I walked over to the computer on the dining room table and picked up a typed page from her doctoral thesis. It read:

The dawn rises as the dough rises,
The dawn lawn grass grows as it rises,
The moon loon rises,
The red sun rises.

I picked up another page and then another. Some of the pages had one word on them. Some had fragments of sentences. None of the pages made any sense.

A copy of D.H. Lawrence's novel *Women in Love* lay next to the computer. I remember Laura telling me how Lawrence thought that ideal lovers should be like two stars orbiting the same hemisphere, holding each other in a magnetic field so that neither sways the other from its course. Star equilibrium, she had said.

In my mind's eye I saw the clear image of one star suddenly pulled away from the other, careening out of control, its brightness fading as it disappeared into the empty darkness of space. I knew at that moment that if I didn't get Laura some help soon, I would be risking not only our relationship, but also her life.

"Red rover," Laura called from upstairs. "Come on over, red rover."

The upstairs was dark except for a small ray of light that shone from Laura's bedroom. She sat naked on her heels on the bed, eyes wide, hands twisting a corner of the sheet that draped across her thighs. A candle on the nightstand burned. Her lips were a glossy red, and they glistened like tears even in the dim light.

My heart pounded, and I suppressed the desire I had for her. I concentrated instead on the birthmark on her side, the dark patch of skin about the size of a quarter that once I saw as unique and now saw as an imperfection.

She smiled a sad, tragic, crazy little smile, and my eyes misted over and something hot and choking welled up into my throat. Tears burned my eyes and trickled down my cheeks. I rubbed the sting and wet away as best I could before she saw, but what remained made my skin feel small and tight, as if it would crack if I moved a facial muscle.

The flame from the candle on the nightstand next to the bed flickered. She lifted an arm, a small hand reached out, lithe fingers beckoned, her shadow on the wall behind her looming as dark as a storm cloud.

I tried to swallow the lump in my throat, tried to forget what I knew in my heart I could never forget.

I turned away and opened a dresser drawer. Her clothes were arranged in small, neat piles. As I pushed a hand through the silk and lace, my mind made a connection between what I was doing to her clothes and what she had done to the two of us, and I began to gain a perverse sense of satisfaction by messing everything up.

"You have to get dressed," I said.

"I don't want to get dressed," she said in a little girl's voice.

I faced her again and said, "You must. Please."

She pulled the sheet up to her chin, covering herself, as if I were an intruder who had broken into her bedroom.

"I'm too stressed . . . to get dressed." She giggled like a child.

"I have a surprise for you."

She brightened. "A surprise? What surprise? I like surprises that are filled with prizes."

"Come along with me and I'll show you."

"I've got to wear a dress," she said. "And a hat. Can't go anywhere without a hat."

"You can wear whatever hat you want," I said.

* * *

I drove her to the hospital on that dark January morning, a morning when the bitter cold frosted the hairs in my nostrils and exhaust fumes became tiny clouds of ice crystals. A north wind snaked through the openings in my coat, raising goose bumps as it slithered along my flesh.

I had called Dr. Dressler before we left Laura's, and he was waiting for us at the hospital when we arrived.

"Hello, Laura," he said.

"What kind of place is this?" she said. "A nice place . . . I'm not staying here . . . I'm having a hell of a good time . . . Oh, I'm so happy, Michael . . . I have to get going . . . I need my red dress, please, and my red shoes and my red purse . . . Oh, and my red hat . . . I need my red hat, Michael . . . I'm happier now than I've ever been . . . I'm one hundred percent better than normal."

"I'll take it from here," Dressler said.

* * *

I wasn't allowed to see Laura the first week, though I went to the hospital daily in hopes that Dressler might change his mind. At night I would come home feeling sick to my stomach, unable to shake the sense of helplessness that stayed with me like the pungent odor of antiseptic.

Laura wasn't in the locked section of the ward, and so, tiring of Dressler's excuses, I walked past the busy nurses' station on Monday of the following week and down a long hallway, peering into open doors, until I found Laura.

I wished I hadn't.

She lay curled like a fetus on a bed. The white of her hospital gown was in stark contrast to her dark, sunken cheeks. Her hair was damp with perspiration, and it clung slickly to her forehead like leeches. And her beautiful eyes—eyes that once had sparkled and danced to the music of life—were like two pieces of stone. They registered nothing.

I turned away and rested my forehead against the cool plaster walls and breathed deeply, trying to swallow the bile that rose in my throat. I wanted to walk over to the bed and take Laura in my arms and hold her and tell her how much I loved her, but the sight of her repulsed something inside me. I hated myself for feeling the way I did, hated myself more than I ever thought I could, and still I couldn't bring myself to touch her.

I turned toward her again and leaned against the wall. I could see the end of the bed and the medical chart that was clipped on the foot rail. I could see the name written on the chart, and what I saw made me blink.

LAURA SEATON AUBREY

I read it a second time, but it still said the same thing.

* * *

"Do you have an appointment?" Stephen Dressler's receptionist said when I stormed into the waiting room.

"No, I don't," I replied, brushing past her. I shoved open Dressler's door, and it banged against the doorstop. Dressler was sitting behind his desk, reading some papers.

"I'm sorry, Doctor," the receptionist said over my shoulder, "but he—"

"That's all right, Susan," Dressler said calmly. He stood up. "I'll see Mr. Collins now."

She left the room and closed the door behind her.

"Why the hell didn't you tell me Laura was related to Alexander Seaton?" I said.

"I thought you knew she was his granddaughter."

"I told you before Laura didn't talk much about her family."

"Why don't you sit down?" he said.

"I don't want to sit down. And I don't want any goddamn tea either. I want Laura out of there."

"I'm afraid we can't do that."

"Who are *we*?"

He gestured with his hand toward the leather chair in front of his desk. "Please."

"You can't keep her there against her will."

"I'm not. Admission papers have been signed. We can keep her for as long as six months."

"Who signed the papers?" When Dressler didn't respond, I said, "I'll get a court order. I'll get her out."

"You know that wouldn't be in Laura's best interests."

"Dammit!" I said. "I should never have listened to you."

"If you'll let me explain, I think you'll understand."

"Understand what? That Laura doesn't know what the hell has happened to her, that I trusted you? That she trusted me?" My voice and hands trembled with anger and frustration.

"Laura's going to be all right. Believe me."

I jammed my hands into the pockets of my overcoat, trying to stop myself from shaking.

"Please," he said again, offering me the chair.

"I don't want to sit down. Just tell me what's happened to Laura!"

"Laura's in an extremely depressed state."

I gave a derisive laugh. "Thanks for the astute diagnosis."

He sat down in the chair behind his desk, seemingly unperturbed. "You did the right thing by bringing her to the hospital."

"That's easy for you to say. Have you seen her recently?" After I said it, I realized how stupid a question it was.

"Of course. I was hoping you could wait."

"I can see why. When I brought her to the hospital, at least she could talk."

"When you brought her in, Laura was in a highly manic state. Pressured speech, clang associations—"

"Cut the clinical crap."

"Sorry. Her speech patterns were typical of a manic state, with compulsive rhyming or alliteration. We began treating her with lithium. It normally takes about ten days to two weeks to work. But after three days she lapsed into a depressed state. We switched to antidepressants, but again, they take time to become effective. We may have to use ECT to bring her out of it more quickly."

I leaned forward and placed my hands on his desk, palms down. "You don't mean shock therapy."

"Let me dispel some myths, Mr. Collins. ECT has a higher success rate for severe depression than any other form of treatment."

"I don't want her to have the shock treatments. Anything else, but not shock treatments."

"I assure you, Mr. Collins, this isn't *One Flew Over the Cuckoo's Nest.* Laura will be put to sleep. A very small current is passed through the brain. Because she's anesthetized, she'll sleep peacefully through it all."

"And what happens when she comes out of it?"

"Sometimes there's a brief period of confusion, headache or muscle stiffness, but these symptoms typically ease in a matter of twenty minutes to an hour."

"What if Laura isn't typical? What if she ends up in an insane asylum like her mother?"

"We prefer to call them mental health centers," he said.

"Call them what you like, Doctor. Tell me. What guarantee do I have that Laura won't end up like her mother?"

"I can't give you a guarantee. What I can assure you of is that with today's advances, Laura stands a good chance of living a relatively normal life as long as she takes her prescribed drugs."

"So you say, Doctor."

He opened a desk drawer and took out a pad and a pencil and jotted down a telephone number and address. "Let me give you some information on a support group here in town for friends and relatives of patients who suffer from bipolar disorder."

"Support?" I said. "I'm not the one who needs the support."

He tore a page off the pad and handed it across the desk to me. "These people have gone through what you're going through. I'm certain they can help alleviate your concerns, help you cope with Laura's disorder."

I glanced at the writing on the paper. "That's it?"

"For now," he said.

"Thanks a hell of a lot for all the information."

"There is one other thing," he said.

"What?"

He looked at me for what seemed like a long time.

"What?" I said a second time, but with more of an edge.

"If you would like to talk further, Mr. Collins."

"Talk? All I've done is talk, and still you wouldn't tell me anything about Laura. I had to find out she was related to Alexander Seaton from her medical chart. What makes you think I'd want to talk with you about her again?"

"Not about Laura."

"What then?"

He didn't respond.

"I hate that," I said. "Why won't you just come out and say what it is you have to say?"

"Why won't you?"

"I'm out of here."

"Mr. Collins," he called as I reached the door.

I hesitated.

"You need to be patient. Everything will work out in time."

"I'd like to believe that, Doctor. I really would." I stuffed the paper in my coat pocket and walked out of his office.

* * *

The sky was overcast and the wind gusted and swirled, creating miniature tornadoes of snow as I got in my car. Though I had refused to admit it, ever since Laura had told me that her mother was in an institution, the idea of visiting her had lingered in my subconscious like a nightmare. I had to know, despite my trepidation, if what I feared, if what I saw in the black hole of sleep was, in fact, reality.

I drove seventy-five miles south, past a flat white landscape of farms and fields, to the state mental institution in the small town of St. Clair. The town itself was limited to one main street, with a cafe, a hardware store, a feed supply, a John Deere dealership, a movie theater showing a year-old movie, a grocery store with a couple of gas pumps in front of it, and a Dairy Queen. The institution was a mile south of town, according to the signs. It sat on about ten acres of land, high on a hill, the three brick buildings rising like faulted mountains out of the prairie. A long, tarred road, which wound through oak and maple trees stripped bare by the hands of winter, led up to the visitors' parking lot and the main entrance. I was surprised to see that there wasn't a fence around the institution.

As I got out of my car, I realized that I might not be able to see Laura's mother, that I might have to bluff my way in, pretend to be someone I wasn't. But I had arrived during visiting hours, and the staff proved to be friendly and accommodating.

"You're the first person that's come to see Mrs. Aubrey in years," a heavyset nurse said as she led me down a narrow corridor. She carried a set of large keys on a ring that struck her thigh as we walked, and the sound echoed like we were in a cave. There was a strong smell of ammonia in the air and an odd quiet about the place, as if those that were here were not really here at all, but in some unique and distant place of their own choosing.

We walked towards a man mopping the corridor. He looked up and smiled as we walked by him. He wore gray coveralls and a Twins baseball cap pulled on so tightly as to make it seem too small for his head. He had large ears and the face of a boy trapped in a man's body.

"Hullo," he said in a deep voice.

"Hello, Joey," the nurse replied.

I was uncomfortable. Sadness was part of it. That I could understand. But I was feeling something else here, something I didn't want to feel, and yet I couldn't help myself. And that feeling made me uneasy, made me want to leave, to run as fast as I could and to breathe clean, fresh air.

"Here we are, Mr. Collins," the nurse said.

Laura's mother was sitting in a wheelchair in her windowless room, head tilted slightly, looking at the bare white walls. Pale and thin, she wore a pink bathrobe and slippers. Her graying hair was done up in a bun. Distended blue veins cut a jagged path between the liver spots on her hands.

I sat down in a hardback chair next to her.

Her eyes were the same color as Laura's, though her mother's lids drooped and there was an area of white under her irises, as if they were floating in a milky sea. But it was her emptiness that I sensed most strongly; the feeling that her spirit had left her body and all that remained was a hollow shell.

"My name's Michael," I said. "I'm a friend of Laura's."

Her breathing was slow, and as she exhaled, I smelled the rank odor of her breath.

The heavyset nurse standing in the doorway said, "Mrs. Aubrey hasn't spoken since she arrived, Mr. Collins. She's catatonic."

I sat there for a minute, stunned, trying to get a sense of what I was feeling. Echoes of a line from a Dickinson poem reverberated in my mind, a poem read only once on an airplane bound for St. Thomas, but a poem remembered because I would always associate it with Laura.

A quartz contentment like a stone.

I hadn't understood the poem or the line from it at the time, but now, as I looked at Laura's mother, I knew what Dickinson meant.

A quartz contentment like a stone.

And then I realized quite suddenly that what I had felt walking down the hallway, that what I felt now, was fear. I stood and backed away from Laura's mother.

"Are you all right, Mr. Collins?" the nurse asked.

"I'm sorry," I muttered, stumbling past her and out into the corridor. "I didn't know." I ran down the corridor, ran as fast as my legs would carry me, as if any moment the doors would lock, and I would be trapped and forced to stay.

On my way back to the city, I couldn't stop thinking about the hurtful things Laura had said and done. But most of all, I couldn't quell the voice that warned, *In twenty years you could be standing in an institution, looking at Laura and feeling that same sense of fear and revulsion.*

I drove nearly fifty miles before I took the piece of paper with the phone number and address for the support group Dr. Dressler had given me out of my coat pocket. I looked at it till the letters and numbers blurred. Then I opened the driver's side window, held the paper in the wind, and let it go.

*   *   *

As twilight glows like coals through the windows of my apartment, I put Laura's wrinkled photograph back in my wallet and stare at the beer in the glass in front of me. I watch the tiny bubbles of gas float from the bottom to the top of the glass and listen to the words that keep repeating endlessly inside my head.

If I ever get sick, I want you to promise you'll take care of me.

I promise.

I want you to mean it, Michael. Not just say it.

I do mean it.

Say it again.

I promise I'll take care of you, Laura.

I drink the last of the beer in the glass.

Chapter 18

At six a.m. I reach over and turn down the volume on the radio. I remain in bed for a time, staring up at the ceiling at a fly entangled in a spider's web. The fly's not dead yet, and it continues to struggle, moving its legs and wings in a desperate attempt to free itself.

I don't remember having slept, though I must have dozed off toward morning. My head aches from the beer I drank the night before, and my mouth feels pasty and dry, as if I have lint on my tongue. The room is hot, the bed sheet damp with perspiration. A disc jockey announces that the temperature is already eighty degrees. I need a shower and some idea as to how to approach the day. The shower will be the easy part.

I take a moment to examine my neck in the bathroom mirror. Though it's still sore where Jack's fingernails dug into the skin, the red marks have faded considerably, and there doesn't appear to be any permanent damage. I wonder how long it'll take before the marks disappear completely.

I feel refreshed for about five minutes after my shower. By the time I finish shaving and put on a pair of slacks and a shirt, I'm sweating again from the humidity. I have a hot dog and a glass of orange juice for breakfast. Then I head for my car.

The early morning sky is the color of sulfur. Broken white clouds are scattered about, as if God, in a fit of anger, has torn them up like scraps of paper. A thin layer of fog rises like steam off boiling water.

I get to school about 7:15, pulling in beside a flatbed with a crane and wrecking ball on it. Jack Stone's pickup is parked in the faculty lot. I consider returning home and calling in sick but decide it's too late for that. It's too late for a lot of things.

Still, I enter the building through the farthest door from the main office and slip unnoticed into my room. I dread having to go to the lounge, and I wonder if Mac Tyler will check my mailbox for me. One look across the hall reveals that Mac, a notoriously late arriver, isn't in his room yet.

I spend fifteen minutes rearranging the papers and books on my desk. It isn't that I'm afraid of Jack Stone. I find it hard to believe that he would attempt to strangle me in school. It's more a fear of the unknown, of wondering exactly how Jack will react when we see each other today. Then again, I think, Jack may want to avoid me as much as I want to avoid him. He may feel embarrassed, even remorseful—though somehow I doubt it—about what has happened.

I have a fleeting wish that something would happen to Jack, an accident, perhaps, or a rare disease. I picture myself in a hastily called faculty meeting chaired by the somber superintendent of the school district.

We thought the disease was confined to the tropics. How poor Jack contracted it is a mystery.

If the district has to hire a new principal, I still might be offered Kate Fleming's job. Then, chastising myself for having such a thought, I force myself to think of something else.

Five minutes before homeroom, when the halls are crowded with noisy students, I walk down to the lounge and check my mailbox. I keep waiting to bump into Jack, to see him standing in the hallway. Then I remember that he dislikes being in the hallway at the same time as the students. Actually, Jack dislikes being in the building at the same time as the students.

My heart races along as if I had three cups of coffee for breakfast. For a moment I consider walking over to the office and saying, "Hi, Jack," just to release my tension and find out what, if anything, Jack is going to do—but only for a moment.

A checklist of the final days' procedures is attached to Friday's bulletin. The sheet reminds me that I have to complete my report cards and turn in my grade book, my overhead projector, my teacher's handbook, and a list of any students who have failed before I can collect my last paycheck. In the past I'd have had an extra day or two to hand in my materials, but because the building is scheduled to be razed next week, today is the staff's, as well as the students', last day at Wilson. Few are complaining.

I hurry back to my homeroom, where I take attendance and listen as Elaine Samuels, Jack's secretary, reads the morning announcements over the loudspeaker. The seniors in my homeroom are preoccupied with discussing the night's graduation ceremonies.

Ann Robbins, Danny O'Brien's girlfriend, brings her yearbook up to my desk right before homeroom ends and proudly shows me a picture of her and Danny taken at the prom, he in a tux, she in a black gown. As I write a few words underneath the picture, she asks if I've heard anything from Danny.

"No. I haven't."

"I'm worried about him, Mr. Collins. He's missing his finals. He won't graduate." Her eyes are bloodshot, and I wonder if she's been crying.

"We'll get everything made up. He'll be okay."

"I hope so."

I hope so, too, but I say, "I'm sure Danny's fine. He'll show up soon."

During second period, I turn on the window fan in my room to high, hoping to keep the temperature bearable as the students labor over their final reading exams. Trying to keep cool is an exercise in futility.

Mac Tyler comes by my room at lunchtime. "Hot enough for you?"

"I don't need a health club membership. I've got my own sauna right here."

"You want something to eat?"

"I don't think so."

He nods. "Heard anything about Danny O'Brien?"

"You got a minute?"

"Sure do," he replies, squeezing into a desk.

"Danny came to see me at my apartment two nights ago. It was late, and he was pretty confused and upset. He said he needed to talk. I tried to persuade him to call home and let his mother know that he was okay, but he refused. He told me he'd leave if I called. So we talked, and he said that he felt responsible for his parents' divorce. He wanted to get into engineering school at the university to prove to his father and himself that he could be an academic success. And if he didn't pass Bruder's English final, he didn't know what he'd do. I told Danny that he shouldn't put so much pressure on himself, but I wasn't very convincing. I told him I'd drive him to school in the morning, and I let him stay the night. But when I woke up the next morning, he was gone. I haven't seen him since. That was two days ago."

Mac stroked his beard and said, "Danny's a good kid. He'll be okay."

"I wish I could be sure of that."

"Me, too," Mac says. He starts to get up.

"There's something else, Mac." I can feel my stomach tighten as I try to sort out what I'm about to say next.

Mac sits down again.

I decide to come right out with it. "Jack caught me with Nicole the other night. He tried to strangle me." I pointed to my neck, as if for clarification.

"Damn. Were the two of you . . .?"

"No. Remember, I went there to break it off."

"It probably doesn't matter much to Jack at this point."

"You're right. Needless to say, I don't think his job offer still stands."

Mac shakes his head slowly. "I'm sorry, Mike. What're you going to do?"

"I'll tell you what I'm not going to do. I'm not going to ask Jack for a recommendation."

"Wouldn't be a good idea. Have you talked to Jack since it happened?"

"I saw him at Kate Fleming's funeral. I told him it was over. He seemed to feel it wasn't."

"Has he threatened you?"

"You mean outside of trying to strangle me?"

Mac smiles.

"I don't know if you could call what he said at the funeral a threat. But could you blame him?"

Mac looks at me without speaking.

Suddenly feeling uncomfortable, I say, "Maybe I should get out of teaching?" I intend it to be a statement, but it comes out sounding like a question.

"Is that what you think, Mike?"

"What does it matter?"

Mac shrugs. "Maybe in the end, what you think is all that really does matter."

* * *

During sixth period, Beth Stanton peeks in my room and motions me into the hall.

"Congratulations, Michael. I heard you were offered Kate's job." There's no resentment in her voice.

"Yes, Beth. Thanks." *Did you also hear I've been sleeping with Jack's wife?*

"Are you planning on attending the graduation ceremonies this evening?"

"I haven't thought much about it."

"Well," she says, "why don't you think about it?"

"All right."

She starts to turn around to walk back to her room when she pauses and says, "What happened to your neck?"

"It's a rash from shaving. Either that or I'm allergic to something."

"I hope it's not me," she says with a smile.

I smile back.

"If you decide you're going to the graduation ceremonies, let me know. We can go together if you'd like."

I don't know what to say.

"You look surprised," she says.

"Not really."

"Sure you are. But that's okay. Just let me know."

"I'll do that."

She smiles again, returns to her room, and closes the door.

* * *

I sit alone in front of the fan in my room during the last period of the day. I finish correcting my final exams and fill out my report cards, and then I gaze out a window at the western horizon. The air feels muggy, as if I'm sitting in a rain cloud. If it storms, graduation ceremonies will have to be held in the auditorium instead of out on the football field. Since there are only so many seats indoors, that will limit attendance. And the old auditorium isn't air-conditioned.

My mind drifts back to when I was young and practicing on the neighborhood field behind my house with my brother and father, just the three of us, working on pick off throws until dusk, then walking home together in the cool evening air, our bodies aching; Rick telling jokes, making us laugh; Dad smiling, proud of his sons.

And then I'm in Little League, running after a foul pop up, crashing into the wire fence around the field, opening my eyes to see my father's concerned face hovering over me, asking me if I was all right, and me worrying about holding onto the ball, getting the third out.

So many fields through all of the years, each one with a little different character; fields that were dry and dusty and hard, that ripped the flesh off your hips when you slid, where bounces were never true; and others that were soft and moist and smooth, where the sweetness of the grass lingered in your nostrils like the scent of expensive perfume. How many hours had I spent on those fields? How had each one of them shaped and defined my character?

"Please excuse the interruption," the loudspeaker blares. "There will be no after-school activities. All students are requested to leave the building after class. Anything left in lockers will be sent to the district lost and found."

I look around my classroom at the bookshelves, at the dartboard with the target word for the week, REMINISCE: to recollect and tell of past experiences or events. I thought it might be a good word for the seniors on their last day. Perhaps, subconsciously, I was also thinking of myself.

* * *

It took about a week after my trip to the state institution in St. Clair to visit Laura's mother before I realized what I had done. In a panic, I called the hospital where Laura had been admitted to ask about her condition.

"I'm sorry, sir," the receptionist said. "We have no one here named Laura Aubrey."

"Try Seaton," I said.

"No, sir. No one by that name either."

"She has to be there," I said. "She has to."

"I'm sorry, sir."

I disconnected and called Stephen Dressler's office.

"The doctor is in session now. I'll have him call you."

I remembered Susan, Dressler's receptionist, and I was certain she remembered me from the week before when I had stormed into the office. "Please," I said. "As soon as he's free."

"Of course." Her tone was cool.

"It's very important."

"I'll give him the message."

"Thank you," I said, hoping my politeness now would make up for my behavior last week.

It took three agonizing hours before Dressler returned my call.

"What's happened to Laura?" I said.

"Calm down, Mr. Collins. Nothing has happened to her. As a matter of fact, her condition is improving."

"Where is she?"

"She's merely been moved to a better facility."

"Where?"

He didn't reply.

"Come on, Dressler! Where the hell is she?"

"Laura needs some stability in her life right now. Someone who can take care of her."

"It's Seaton, isn't it?" I said. "Seaton's had her moved."

"It's for the best."

"The hell it is!" I said, breaking off the call.

* * *

The only safe way out to Seaton's house on the island in the middle of Dakota Lake in winter was by wind sled. The sled was a small, flat-bottom barge with steel runners under it. A tank engine powered it. A three-bladed propeller was mounted on a huge tripod in the back of the sled. Seven desperate or crazy people could sit under a canopy made of canvas with clear plastic windows. The sled had a gas tank, compass, and headlights, and was steered by a large rudder just aft of the engine. It was used primarily for carrying supplies and mail to the island.

That afternoon I introduced myself to Hank Ketchum, sled driver extraordinaire. Hank piloted the ferry to the island in summer. Before that he had been a barge captain and had been on water for most of his fifty-seven years.

"Sled's much safer than a snowmobile," he said, "but she rides a bit rough on ice." He handed me a pair of earplugs. "Best you wear these."

Hank wore a snowmobile suit, heavy boots nearly up to his knees, thick mittens with liners, and a red flannel hat with earflaps. I wore a down jacket, ski gloves, a pair of Frye boots, and a wool stocking cap. I probably would have looked good on the cover of *GQ*, but Hank was probably much warmer.

The sled had no springs, and the earplugs barely drowned out the roar of the engine. Communication between us was limited to smiles and an occasional gesture of contempt for the fifteen-minute ride. I wondered what would happen if we hit a patch of open water, but Hank had assured me that the sled would float.

A dozen houses were tucked in the secluded bays on the island that was about ten miles long and five miles across. Alexander Seaton lived in a large Queen Anne-style home visible from where we docked. The house stood on a point overlooking the lake. It had a chimney, a turret, and a verandah with a gazebo at one end.

Though it was only two in the afternoon, a pewter gray sky hung low over the water. The old-fashioned street lamps on the island glowed with a dim light. A needle-like wind pricked my face as I walked up the main road. It was covered with patches of ice that made the footing treacherous and the half-mile walk twice as long. My frustration and anger began to dissolve like melting snow.

I wished it was warmer, wished I was in Florida for spring training, which was less than a month away. Spring training. I hadn't thought much about it. How could I take care of Laura if I was in Florida? How could I take care of Laura if I couldn't find her? What made me think that Alexander Seaton would even agree to see me, let alone tell me where she was being treated?

Twenty minutes from the harbor, I stood shivering on the shoulder of the road and stared down the long driveway that led to Seaton's house. The driveway might have been a hundred yards long; it might have been a hundred miles. I had no feeling in my fingers and toes now, no feelings at all.

* * *

The janitors have left me a few empty cardboard boxes in my room. I begin filling them with textbooks and items from my desk. Sweat drips off me as I work.

I have the feeling of it all being something I have been through before and have to go through again, like watching a rerun on television. I had hoped that this year would be different, that finally I had found a secure teaching position. And it would have been secure if I hadn't gotten involved with Nicole Stone. Why? Why had I let myself?

I finish cleaning out my desk and move on to a file cabinet, stacking the thick manila files so I can carry them down to the counseling office. The files are filled with case studies, psychological reports, and yearly individual educational plans on each of my students dating back to when they were first enrolled in special education. Some files go as far back as elementary school and are as thick as dictionaries.

As I stack the files on my desk, I come across Danny O'Brien's. I want to believe that I haven't let him down. I want to believe that I've done all I can for him.

"Excuse me." A guy with a hard hat stands in the doorway to my room, peering in.

"Yes?"

"Just looking things over," he says with a smile. "Don't worry. We're not going to raze the building with the kids in it."

I hear footsteps above me on the roof. "What about the teachers?"

He gives me a look indicating he thinks I'm serious.

"Just kidding."

He smiles again and backs out of the doorway. "Sorry for the bother." He tips his hat and leaves.

I start packing a little faster and consider what I'll do if I can't teach. I assumed when I gave up baseball that somehow, somewhere, I would be able to find a teaching position. Now, after what happened with Nicole, I have to think about alternatives.

What am I going to do with the rest of my life?

I can work for my father. No, I don't think that I can. Besides, I like working with kids. Jack Stone isn't going to write me a letter of recommendation, but Mac will. I can go out of state. It's an option worth considering. There are other options, of course. I have the rest of my life to think about them. But suddenly, without teaching, the rest of my life seems like an awfully long time.

The bell rings, ending school for the day—and the year—and for that old building, forever. I stand outside my door, monitoring the hall, watching and waving to students as they hustle toward the buses. Some are crying and hugging, most are smiling and laughing. I wish for a moment that I were back in high school.

I step back into my room when the halls clear and spend an hour boxing up the last of my materials. I carry my files to the counseling office and then take the overhead projector up to the library and check it in. The old building is oddly quiet.

Notebook papers lie scattered in the halls. Rows of lockers are open and empty. Staff members pack and tape boxes in their rooms.

As I come to Ted Bruder's room, I stop and peer in. Bruder sits hunched over his desk, writing intently in his grade book. I imagine myself charging into the room and tearing up his grade book, but that wouldn't change anything. Danny O'Brien would still be missing, I would still be out of a job, and Bruder would still be an asshole.

"Oh, Collins," Bruder says, looking up from his paperwork.

His voice startles me.

"About that incident the other day concerning Daniel O'Brien. Perhaps . . ." He pauses a moment. "Perhaps I overreacted by going to Mr. Stone."

"Perhaps you did."

"No hard feelings," he says with smile. "After all, the staff has to stick together."

"Uh-huh."

"Did you know that the boy didn't show up for his English final?"

"You mean Danny O'Brien."

"Of course."

"I knew."

"It's frustrating, isn't it?"

"What is?"

"Well, you put so much time and effort into helping a boy like that, and he disappoints you."

"That's how you see it, huh?"

"I've been in this business nearly thirty years, and I've come to expect certain disappointments. It's part of the job. You can't save every one of them. If you want to stay with it for the long haul, my advice is to buck up, learn to live with disappointment."

"Is that so?"

"Best advice I can give you. By the way, have you turned in your room key yet?"

"No. Why would I turn in my key? The building is being razed."

"Because we've always done it that way."

"Things change."

"Some things," he says. "Would you mind dropping off my key in the main office?"

"Yes, I would mind." I leave him sitting at his desk with his mouth open and head down the hallway, where I run into Elaine Samuels.

"Is Jack in his office?" I ask.

"Yes. Sounds like you'll be back full-time next fall. Congratulations."

Apparently Jack hasn't said anything to her—yet.

"Thanks," I reply, not knowing what else to say.

I leave Elaine and walk toward the main office. Halfway down the hallway, I meet Mac Tyler.

He extends a hand. "Mike," he says with a warm smile.

I shake Mac's big, calloused hand.

"You need a job this summer, you come and see me at the cycle shop."

"I will, Mac."

"Regardless, you keep in touch. Let me know where you land."

I nod.

We stand there looking at each other a moment, and I realize how much I'm going to miss him.

"Well," he says.

We shake hands again.

"Take care, Mike."

"You, too."

"You're a helluva good teacher. Whatever happens, remember that."

"Thanks, Mac."

He nods and waves and walks away.

I wonder if I'll ever see him again. How many times in our lives do we promise to stay in touch with someone and never follow through? I really don't know why.

My pulse increases as I reach the main office and walk in. Jack Stone's door is closed. I stare at the door, at the lettering on the outside that reads PRINCIPAL. My mouth feels dry. I can't leave without saying something to Jack, without trying to explain somehow.

I walk over to Jack's door, reach for the doorknob, and then retract my hand, as if I'm about to touch a live wire. I have to get control of my emotions; I have to think of something to say. I take two deep breaths and knock softly.

When there's no answer, I knock again, harder.

"Come in," Jack says. His voice sounds unusually tentative.

I put my hand on the cool metal knob and turn it. The door swings open.

Jack Stone is sitting stiffly behind his desk. His bald head glistens with sweat. His face displays no emotion, but his brown eyes look at me pleadingly.

Danny O'Brien stands behind Jack. Danny's eyes, too, are looking directly at mine. But in Danny's blue eyes I see panic, as if he were a trapped animal looking for someplace to run.

"Danny," I say, stepping forward.

It's then that I see the gun that Danny O'Brien is holding, pointed at the back of Jack Stone's head.

Chapter 19

"Close the door," Danny says, his voice shaking like the gun in his hand.

I step back and shut the door quietly.

"I'm sorry you got involved in this, Mr. Collins," Danny says. "But now that you're here, you'll have to go up to see Bruder with us."

I don't know what to say to Danny, and yet I know I better say something--and it better be good. "Think about what you're doing, Danny," I reply, keeping the panic out of my voice. "Please. Bruder is not worth destroying your life over. Believe me."

"This isn't just about Bruder."

"I know. And I know you're hurting, that you've been hurting for a long time. But there are other ways of working this out with your father." *As if I had worked it out with my father.*

"No," Danny says.

The room feels warm and stuffy, like I'm standing in a closet. The ends of red hair that curl over the collar of Danny's jean jacket are wet with perspiration. I have to keep him talking, have to keep him calm. My gaze shifts from Danny to Jack Stone a moment. *Would Danny really shoot?*

"We'd better get going," Jack says, as if reading my thoughts.

I glance at Danny again, at the gun that looks so cold, so deadly in his hand. My mind races with thoughts. I have no idea what to do. I just know that I have to act before something tragic happens.

"We can't go upstairs to see Bruder," I say, more to Jack than to Danny.

"What do you mean?" Jack replies, his voice betraying his distress. "Are you forgetting who has the gun? And how the hell did he get *my* gun in the first place?"

Danny looks quickly at Jack.

"I'm not forgetting. But I also remember who's responsible for this situation." Speaking to Danny, I say, "I'll go up to Bruder's room with you. Leave Mr. Stone here. He's got nothing to do with this."

"For crissakes, Collins," Jack says, glaring at me. "What're you trying to be, a hero?"

I see the deep scratches on the back of Jack's hands where Nicole's fingernails dug into his skin as she pried his hands from around my throat.

"I'm no hero, Jack."

"No. I think we both know what you are."

A current of guilt runs through me. "Look, Jack, all I'm saying is that Danny's my responsibility."

"I think you should just shut the hell up, Collins, and let the kid do what he wants."

Someone knocks on the door, and my heart falls into my shoes.

"Mr. Stone?" Elaine Samuels calls. "Are you in there?"

The door bumps against my back as Elaine tries to push it open all the way.

She pokes her head in the room. "What's going on?" Then, seeing the gun in Danny's hand, she lets out a shriek and retreats, pulling the door closed with a slam.

Danny's wide eyes stare at me, a look of terror on his face.

One of the extension lights on Jack Stone's phone blinks on. I know whom Elaine Samuels is calling. And I also know that there is little time to save Danny. I take one step toward him.

He points the gun at me and backs up abruptly, away from Jack Stone, into the corner of the room. Danny's skin pales, his breathing more rapid.

My heart thumps harder in my chest.

"What the hell are you doing?" Jack says. His lips are tensed. The swivel chair he is sitting in rolls against the wall behind him as he stands.

"Give me the gun, Danny," I say, ignoring Jack. I hold out my left hand.

Danny runs his tongue over his lips.

"Don't be stupid, Collins," Jack says.

"You're not going to shoot me, are you, Danny?" I say, unsure if I actually believe what I'm saying.

Danny says nothing. He stands stiffly in the corner of the room and holds the gun in both hands with the barrel pointing straight at my chest.

"Let me handle this, Collins," Jack says. "You don't have to prove anything to me."

Keeping my eyes fixed on Danny, I say, "I'm not trying to prove anything. I already know what you think of me. I don't intend to let Danny ruin his life."

Jack moves his jaw, as if chewing his words.

I take one small step forward. I maintain eye contact with Danny rather than with the barrel of the gun, which appears as wide as the mouth of a cave.

"Don't come any closer, Mr. Collins," he says in a quavering voice.

My legs feel weak and my throat dry.

"Jesus, Collins," Jack mutters. "Stay where you are."

There's a dull ache in the center of my chest, as if from the impact of a bullet.

"Son," Jack says to Danny, "listen to me."

Danny half turns to his right, so that he can still keep his eyes and the gun on me and see Jack Stone at the same time.

Between the slats of the Venetian blinds behind Jack, I see the flashing red lights of the three squad cars that come to a stop at the curb.

"If you'll give this up now, son," Jack continues, "I promise we'll get this mess with Mr. Bruder straightened out. Won't we, Collins?"

Somewhat taken aback, but nonetheless heartened by Jack's proposal, I manage a hesitant, "Sure."

"And the school won't press charges," Jack adds. "You have my word on it."

Danny appears to be having difficulty holding the gun steady, even with two hands. I fear that it might discharge accidentally.

The phone on Jack's desk buzzes, and my heart skips. I have all I can do to keep from sinking to my knees.

"Who's that?" Danny blurts. He looks at me, then at Jack, then at me again.

"Probably the police," I say.

"The police?" Jack says irritably. He turns and peers out the windows behind him.

"Please, Danny," I say. I take one more step forward as Danny's gaze follows Jack's. "I know you don't want to hurt anyone."

The gun barrel is now a foot from my chest. My hands are down at my sides, and I wonder if I have the strength to lift them, or the courage to take the gun out of Danny's hands.

"Should I answer the phone?" Jack says to no one in particular.

We all watch the blinking phone light and listen to the incessant buzzing.

"Well?" Jack says, looking at Danny.

Danny shrugs.

The buzzing stops.

The room is quiet. Perspiration dampens my shirt. The freckles on Danny's face appear enlarged, as though I'm seeing them through a magnifying glass.

I lift my hands slowly while keeping my eyes locked on Danny's, trying to project as much sensitivity and compassion as I can. Carefully, I place my hands around the gun barrel. It feels cold to the touch. I force myself to smile as I push the gun to my right, away from my chest, and gently pull on it, hoping that Danny will let go. Though the phone no longer buzzes, there's a similar sound in my ears.

I put the palm of my left hand over the barrel, as if that would stop a bullet. "It's okay, Danny." I can feel his resistance, his reluctance to give up the gun. My skin is hot and tingling. Sweat drips down my cheek. I can see Danny's finger on the curve of the trigger. I will myself not to close my eyes.

No one moves.

In that moment that seems to go on forever, I have the crazy thought that Danny's eyes have never looked so big and so blue.

"I'm sorry, Mr. Collins," he says. "I'm really sorry." His chin drops to his chest, and he releases his grip on the gun.

Jack Stone lets out an audible sigh.

I hold the gun out in front of me and suddenly feel sick to my stomach.

Jack reaches out and takes the gun from me.

Danny slumps against the radiator along the wall. He looks like he's about to collapse.

Jack slips an arm around Danny's shoulders and holds him up. "It's going to be okay, son."

A wave of relief washes over me and relaxes the tension in my muscles. I step back and lean against the door behind me, suddenly realizing as I inhale that, unconsciously, I've been holding my breath.

Danny puts his head in Jack Stone's chest and sobs.

Jack's eyes are wet. "I meant what I said, Danny." He sets the gun on the desk. It rests beside the picture of his dead son. "We'll get this mess with Mr. Bruder straightened out. And the school won't press charges if I have anything to say about it."

Maybe Jack does like kids after all, I think. I'm surprised that he hasn't reacted angrily to the incident. I wonder if he's thinking about his son, about how he wished he could have saved him, as he has just helped save Danny O'Brien.

We all stand there for a time until finally Danny steps away from Jack and wipes his eyes with the sleeve of his jean jacket.

"I really didn't mean any harm," he says. "The gun wasn't even loaded." He picks it up. "See?"

"Careful," Jack says.

Danny pulls the trigger and the gun fires in a resounding roar, killing Jack Stone instantly.

Chapter 20

I sit at Bob Haber's desk in the assistant principal's office, trying to block out the bright red image of Jack Stone's chest exploding before my eyes, but no matter how many times I force the vivid memory from my mind, it comes screaming back.

I catch fragments of conversations through the numbness that envelopes my body, bits and pieces that I can't follow as police move in and out of the main office. Outside the windows, local television stations have arrived with their minivans and minicams. Reporters mill around on the sidewalk, holding microphones, waiting for someone to come out of the building and tell them exactly what has happened.

Mac Tyler stands in the corner of Haber's office with his hands in his pants pockets, looking out the wall of windows, watching television crews unloading equipment.

I've been sitting at the desk for an eternity, ever since a black plainclothes detective named Monroe began questioning me.

"So you're telling me you took the gun away from the boy," he says, jotting something down on his note pad.

"Pretty stupid, huh?"

"I'd call it something else."

Monroe wears thick glasses, a button-down dark indigo short-sleeve shirt, and a maize necktie with a perfect Windsor knot.

"What's going to happen to Danny?" I ask.

"We'll take him to the station for now."

"He's going to need some help getting through this."

"We'll see what we can do."

"Thanks. Is it all right if I leave now?"

"I've just got one more question," Monroe replies. He's looking down at his shiny right shoe that has a small scuff mark on the toe. He wrinkles his forehead in consternation. "I was wondering," he says, looking at me now, "if you have any idea where Danny O'Brien got the gun?"

"It's Jack's gun," I say without thinking.

"I know that. I ran a check on the registration. What I was wondering is where the boy got the gun?"

I look at Mac. He nods at me as if to say, "Go ahead and tell him."

"Danny took it from my apartment. I didn't know he'd taken it till I walked into Jack's office this afternoon."

"How did you manage to have Jack Stone's gun?"

"Nicole gave it to me the other night."

"Nicole?"

"Jack's wife."

"Why would she give you her husband's gun?"

"Because . . ." I hesitate before continuing. "The more I try to explain it, Detective, the worse it sounds."

The bright office lights hurt my eyes. I squint as my heart thuds in time to the beat of a headache that throbs above my right eye.

"Were you and Mrs. Stone having an affair?" Monroe asks.

"What does that have to do with anything?"

"Maybe nothing. Maybe everything."

"Look, Detective," Mac says. "Jack Stone's death was an accident."

"That's what I'm attempting to establish."

"No you're not."

Monroe says nothing.

"One life's been lost already," Mac continues. "There's no need to destroy anyone else's."

Monroe stares at the *Semper Fi* tattoo on Mac's right forearm. "Were you in Iraq?"

Mac nods.

"Whereabouts?"

Mac was silent for a time before he said, "Fallujah."

"First battle or second?"

"The second."

"Jesus," Monroe mutters. "The bloodiest battle of the war." As Monroe looks at Mac, something passes between them. Monroe glances at me, then at Mac again. "Well," he says, turning his full attention back to me, "you'll have to come to the station and make a statement."

"When?"

"The sooner, the better."

"All right."

Monroe puts his note pad in the pocket of his shirt and looks at Mac once more. Then he turns and strides out of the office.

"Thanks, Mac," I say.

"It wasn't your fault." His voice sounds distant; his words seem to bounce off the walls in the room, echoing till they gradually fade away.

"You don't think Monroe believes I had something to do with Jack's death, do you?"

"No. He's only doing his job. Asking all the questions."

"I never thought to check if Danny took the gun when he left my apartment. Once the police report where Danny got the gun, I suppose the lawyers will be coming out of the woodwork."

"It was Jack's gun," Mac replies, as if offering an alibi. "And it was Nicole who urged you to take it from the house."

"If I hadn't agreed to take the gun, Jack would be alive now. Hell, if I hadn't been sleeping with Nicole, Jack would be alive now."

Mac looks out the windows at Monroe, standing now alongside Bob Haber, who is reading a statement to the press corps. A mob of reporters are taking notes and pushing microphones in Haber's face as they gather around him.

Mac turns and looks at me. "If you hadn't been born, Jack would be alive now."

"Right," I say, more to myself than to Mac.

He crosses his arms and rests his backside against the windowsill. Beyond the glass, Monroe is fielding questions from the group of reporters. "If you want to blame somebody," Mac says, "blame Jack. He left the round in the chamber. He should've known better."

On top of Haber's desk is a framed picture of a much heavier Bob Haber and his attractive wife, a woman with honey-colored hair, brown eyes, and a faintly amused mouth. I recall that they're childless, though Haber has revealed that they've been going to a fertility clinic. My thoughts shift to the framed picture on the desk in Jack Stone's office, the one of Nicole and Jack Jr.

"Remember as a little kid, Mac, when you were really angry with someone. Did you ever wish something bad would happen to them?"

"I think most kids have had that thought at one time or another."

"You really think so?"

"I do."

"What do you think about adults? Adults who wish something would happen to another person?"

Mac steps away from the windows and stands in front of the desk, looking down at me as though I'm a student called down to the office for misbehaving.

"Look, Mike. What happened to Jack was an accident. Now I know it isn't much consolation, and I don't want to burst your bubble, but if you hadn't gotten involved with Nicole Stone, she would've found someone else."

"Still, I never got the chance to talk to Jack, to try and explain why I got involved with Nicole. Not that I completely understand it myself. Or that it would have mattered to Jack, I suppose."

Behind Mac I see a uniformed police officer leading a handcuffed Danny O'Brien out of the main office.

Danny pauses at the door that leads into the hallway and looks back at me. Blood stains the white T-shirt he wears under his jean jacket. His face is expressionless and his eyes are fixed in a blank stare, as if he is still in shock. Yet, as his gaze rests on me, he raises his hands to chest level, splays the fingers of his right hand, and slowly, forming an arc, he waves good-bye.

* * *

I leave the school through one of the side entrances to avoid reporters. As I drive to the police station, I realize I'm shivering even though the temperature is near ninety.

Traffic is heavy through town; lots of people taking off early on a hot, muggy Friday, probably heading out of town for the weekend with their families now that school has ended. I notice Seaton High's baseball field on my left. It's situated in a residential neighborhood behind the modern school building. The playoffs for the high school tournaments have started on diamonds throughout the state.

I pull over.

I park my car next to the curb and walk across the street till I'm standing alone on the third base side next to a five-foot-high chain-link fence that encircles the field. In a breeze as soft as a child's breath, I catch the scent of charcoals burning and beef cooking on a backyard grill.

The scoreboard to my left reads Seaton 3, Hamilton 2, in the top of the fourth inning. I can clearly see the infield and the large crowd seated on the bleachers near the dugouts. A few fans linger against the screen behind home plate.

For a moment I see myself on the mound again, staring in at the catcher, waiting for the sign, concentrating, shutting out everything around me, focusing all my energy on a small target sixty feet six inches away.

And then I'm in the present again, moving out of the blistering sunlight, standing under the shade of an oak tree about five feet from the fence, listening to the buzz of the crowd, the chatter of the outfielders. It's the first baseball game I've attended since I left the Mets' farm club in Florida five years ago.

As I watch the game, I keep seeing flashbacks of the bullet wound that tore open Jack Stone's chest and smelling the sickly odor of his blood.

I turn away from the field and move behind the thick trunk of the oak tree, trying to control my breath that comes in the short gasps you get when you start to cry. My mouth is dry and my skin clammy, and the field begins to whirl in front of me. A kaleidoscope of images flashes in front of my eyes; images of Danny, Jack, my father—Laura.

I slump down on all fours in the grass, muffling the sobs that rack my body. Spasms convulse my stomach, and I vomit. I haven't eaten much and so not much comes up, but it takes quite a while.

"You okay, mister?"

Startled, I look up. The left fielder, a good-looking, muscular kid, is leaning against the inside of the fence. A shiny white baseball rests on the ground outside the fence a couple of feet from me.

"I'm fine," I say, feeling the heat of embarrassment in my face.

"Could you toss me the ball?"

"Sure."

I wipe my eyes and mouth and the mucus from my nose with a handkerchief. Then I pick up the ball and stand up. My legs wobble a second before they feel strong under me.

"Flip it here," he says. "I'll toss it in."

The fingers of my left hand caress the laces and the smooth sheen of horsehide. It's been a long time since I touched a baseball.

"It's okay," I say. "I'll toss it," and with that I rear back and heave the ball in the direction of home plate some three hundred and forty feet away, watching as the ball arcs toward the infield, a white dot against the blue sky, and bounces near the catcher and umpire.

The left fielder gives a low whistle. "Nice arm, man. You ever play any ball?"

I smile and say, "Yes. Yes, I did."

Chapter 21

I arrive at the police station at six o'clock. Lieutenant Monroe is waiting. Once again, I go over what happened in Jack Stone's office. However, this time I tell Monroe in more detail how I got the gun. Then I sign a statement verifying the facts as I recalled them.

As I'm walking out of the office, I nearly bump into Nicole Stone.

"Hello, Michael."

"Hello."

"Are you okay?"

"I've been better. And you?"

"I'm all right."

I didn't expect her to be sobbing uncontrollably over her husband's death, but I thought she might be more upset than she appears. Then again, maybe reality hasn't hit her.

"I'm sorry about Jack," I say. "It was an accident."

She nods. "You know, Jack and I hadn't slept together for nearly two years. Yet now that he's gone, I'll miss him." She looks down at the purse she holds in her hands and then up at me again. She has tears in her eyes now. "I don't think I'll sleep much tonight."

"Me neither."

Her eyes sweep the room and come back to my face. "Would you mind very much if we went somewhere later and had a drink?"

"I'd like to go home now. Can I take a rain check?"

She's about to say something and then hesitates.

Monroe comes out of his office and motions for her. Nicole gives me a tight little smile, turns, and walks into his office.

* * *

It's seven p.m. when I finally return to my apartment. I no sooner open the door than my cell phone rings. I assure my mother and then my brother that I'm all right. Unfortunately, the press continues to call, and at nine o'clock I shut off my phone.

I know I won't sleep. Though my body aches with exhaustion, my mind keeps replaying Jack Stone's death. Not even a beer and hot shower help.

Jack's death is headline news in the papers on Saturday. I want to attend the wake on Sunday and the funeral on Monday, but since I'm an eyewitness to the shooting, I might be too much of a distraction. So I remain locked in my apartment for the weekend, neither showering nor shaving.

Sleep is restless.

I wake in the mornings before sunrise and sit on my fold-out bed in the still darkness and stare out a window. I have time to think—maybe too much—and I spend some of it thinking about Danny O'Brien, wondering how he's handling Jack's death. I call his house a few times, but all I get is an answering machine.

The rest of my time is spent thinking about Jack Stone, and how I never had the chance to tell him that I was sorry for what happened between Nicole and me. Maybe it's guilt and maybe I'm feeling a little sorry for myself, but I still regret never having had the opportunity to explain.

Early Monday evening I leave my apartment, driven finally by a lazy restlessness born out of my self-imposed confinement. I put on a sweat suit and jogging shoes and take my car down to Dakota Lake, where I park and walk, inhaling the clean air in deep gulps, trying to shake the lethargy.

I'm crossing a bridge as dusk settles, watching the ducks paddling around, ignoring the traffic noise and the slight stitch in my side, moving in what generously might be called a slow jog, when I hear a horn honk. A teal Volvo pulls up beside me. An automatic window hums open.

"Michael," Nicole says.

I lean down and rest my forearms on the window frame. "Hi."

"Remember that rain check?"

"I'd like to finish my run and then—"

"No strings. Please, Michael. As a favor to an old lady."

"You're not—"

She places a forefinger on my lips to silence me. "I know I'm not old. I just feel that way tonight."

I don't feel much like making small talk, and so the drive to a restaurant on the other side of the lake is quiet and uneventful, though not particularly uncomfortable.

A waiter seats us at a white, wrought iron table with a CIZANO umbrella on a wooden deck overlooking the yacht club and the lake. I order a Coors and Nicole orders a Johnny Walker and water.

She wears open-toed shoes that could be described as Gucci's version of sandals, and a spring green skirt and a white cotton sweater with green pyramids that perfectly match the skirt. Her hair is down and appears looser, as if she recently washed it. She shivers as a cool breeze blows off the water.

"Cold?" I ask.

She shakes her head.

There's a low buzz of conversation and a tinkle of silverware and glasses coming from the tables around us. I can't help wondering what Nicole wants to talk about, and I can't help thinking that it has something to do with us. I don't like myself much for having that thought, but I'd like Nicole less if it turned out to be true.

We sit quietly at the table for a while before I say, "Did you want to talk about Jack?"

"Yes."

A candle in a red glass on the table gives off a dim light, and it's difficult to read her eyes.

"I wanted to come to the funeral, Nicole, but I thought it might cause a commotion."

"I understand. That's not what I wanted to talk to you about. I was wondering," she says hesitantly, "what happened exactly?"

"Didn't Detective Monroe tell you?"

"I want to hear it from you."

Before I can answer, the waiter brings our drinks. I sip my beer. Nicole doesn't touch her Scotch.

"I went to see Jack to apologize," I say when the waiter departs. "To try and explain why we got involved. Danny O'Brien was already there. I just walked in on them. Eventually Jack and I were able to talk Danny into giving me the gun. I gave it to Jack. He put it on the desk. I thought the incident was over. So did Jack. He was hugging Danny."

"Hugging the boy?"

I nod. "Jack even promised he wouldn't press charges. Then Danny picked up the gun to show us it was empty. He didn't realize there was still a shell in the chamber. Like I said, it was an accident." I drink some beer. Off in the distance I hear the whine of a speedboat. "I think Jack really did like kids, Nicole. Up until his son's death."

She picks up her glass of Scotch and takes a long drink.

"I wish I would've had the chance to explain to him about us."

"What would you have said to him?"

"I don't know exactly. I do know that what we did was wrong. Regardless of what happened between Jack and you."

She sets the glass on the table again. "Did you ever think that maybe we try and make life more complicated than it is, Michael, just to cover up our mistakes?"

"Was it a mistake marrying Jack?"

"I know this might be hard for you to believe, Michael, but I loved Jack once. Then everything changed."

"After your son died."

She nods.

"Why didn't you divorce him?"

"Believe me, I thought about it."

"So what stopped you?"

She drinks some Scotch and stares at me. "I wanted to hurt him."

"Because you blamed him for your son's death."

"Yes."

"A divorce would've hurt him."

"I knew Jack loved me. And by withholding my love within the marriage . . ." She stops abruptly, shakes her head, and lowers her gaze.

I think she wanted to punish Jack as much as hurt him, but I don't say it. Instead, I look out at the dark, smooth surface of the lake and then farther out to the lights on the island where Alexander Seaton lives, isolated, cut off from the rest of the world.

"My life used to be simple," I say. "Playing baseball for a living insulated me. I learned never to let things bother me too much. If I was upset, I went out and ran or threw a baseball as hard as I could. I was so within myself, so self-absorbed, that I never learned how to relate to the world outside the locker room. My life was the world series of clichés. I knew exactly what made me happy and sad. I either won or I lost. And if I lost, I could come back tomorrow. I always got another chance. But real life isn't like that. It's not that simple."

"I've often wondered why you got involved with me, Michael."

"You're attractive. More than attractive."

"That's not why."

"How do you know it isn't?"

"I know, Michael. Try again."

"All right. I never was with anyone like you before."

"That's probably closer to the truth. But there's something more. Something you're not telling me."

I don't say anything for a time. Neither does she. We just sit on opposite sides of the table looking at one another like a couple of poker players calling each other's bluff.

Finally I say, "Maybe I got involved with you because I wanted to get caught."

"What?"

"Maybe I wanted to get caught. Maybe I wanted Jack to catch us."

She draws back from me as though I'm suddenly a threat. "You can't be serious."

"Sure I can." I drink more beer as a fresh breeze blows clean against my face.

"Was I part of your plan of self-destructive behavior?"

"It doesn't matter. It's over. The only thing that matters now is that I feel responsible for Jack's death."

"Jack is responsible for his own death."

"Aren't you at all sorry that he's dead?"

"Of course I'm sorry. He was my husband. But can't you see the irony of the whole situation? Think about it," she says with a laugh that really isn't a laugh at all, but more of a cry. "My husband killed my son. And someone's son killed my husband."

I realize as I sit across the table from her how far apart we are and always have been. And it only compounds the mistake I've made, the regrets that I feel.

"They were both accidents, Nicole."

"More irony," she says and finishes off her Scotch.

"I feel sorry for you."

"Don't, Michael," she says, a bit too loudly. Heads turn in our direction. She leans forward and says more softly but still with sharpness, "I don't want your pity."

"What is it you want?"

She sits back in her chair and looks at the empty glass in her hand. "I want to go home."

"All right. I'll call the waiter and—"

"Michigan," she says. "I want to go home to Michigan and start over. To do what I've always wanted to do." She looks at me again and says quietly, "Do you think one can start over?"

"I'd like to think so."

"How about baseball?" she says. "Do you ever think about going back to baseball?"

"It wouldn't be the same."

"Perhaps it would be better?"

I shake my head. "They call baseball a game, and maybe it is. But it isn't something you can drop for a few years and then go back to. Not at the professional level."

"You're still young."

"But old enough to know better."

She slides a hand across the table and touches mine. There's nothing in the touch; rather it's more a touch of tenderness. "Don't think too badly of me."

"I won't."

"I'm afraid you already do."

I drink the rest of my beer.

"You gave me something I thought I had lost forever," she says. "You gave me hope. And that isn't so bad, is it?"

"No."

"Then is it all right if an older lady gives you some advice?"

"Sure."

"Whatever it is that's troubling you, resolve it, Michael."

"I will."

"Promise?" she says.

"I'm afraid I'm not too good at . . ." I catch myself. I give her hand a squeeze. "Yes. I promise."

Chapter 22

Tuesday is so clear that the only white I can see in the sky is the high-altitude condensation trail left by a jet. I remember when I played ball we used to call it a "high sky" because it was so difficult to pick out the ball against the clear blue background. The temperature hovers around seventy-five, and a gentle breeze blows out of the west.

Collins Trucking is located in northeast Minneapolis on East Hennepin in the warehouse district, not far from the University of Minnesota. I park my car in the gravel lot next to a semi-trailer late that afternoon and walk into the warehouse, which is the size of a small hangar. Inside there are two more trailers and a tractor cab. A mechanic in stained overalls has the hood up and what looks like half the engine parts spread out on the concrete floor next to the cab. The air smells strongly of grease and oil.

In the background I hear the steady hum of traffic and the twang of country music coming from a radio near the truck. Other than the mechanic, the place appears deserted. But I know as I head for the office in the back corner that as long as the warehouse is open, my father will be here.

I can see him now through the dusty glass office window, sitting alone at his desk, reading what is probably an invoice. For a moment I consider turning around and leaving. But my father has never understood why I walked away from baseball, walked away on the day I was headed for the major leagues, walked out of the clubhouse after talking with my manager, Johnny Desmond, supposedly on my way to New York, and instead took a flight home. Maybe I've never clearly understood why either. I realize that if we don't talk soon, we never will.

When I open the office door, he glances up; then he peers down at the sheet of paper in his hand again, his face expressionless.

I close the door behind me. There are four desks in the office: one for my father, one for my brother, Rick, and two others for the secretaries. On the secretaries' desks are IN and OUT baskets, ashtrays littered with lipstick-stained cigarette butts, half-empty Styrofoam coffee cups, white sugar envelopes, and a jar of Coffee-mate. Computers sit on metal carts behind the desks. A calendar on one wall pictures a busty young blonde in a tight T-shirt and shorts, posing beside a Mack truck.

"Dad," I say.

He continues concentrating on the invoice.

"We need to talk."

Now he looks up, waiting.

"We've needed to talk for as long as I can remember."

"About what?" he says impassively.

"About us. About what's been keeping us apart these last five years. About how we can know each other all of our lives and still be strangers." I move away from the door and walk over to a wooden chair and sit down across the desk from him. "Nothing you say is going to make me angry, Dad. Nothing is going to make me leave till I've said what I have to say."

He puts the invoice on the desk. "I don't want to fight. I'm ready to listen."

I take a deep breath and let it out slowly. "You've never forgiven me for quitting baseball. I understand that. But what you've never understood is why I quit. And maybe I never understood it either."

He ponders my words a minute. Then he rises from his chair and walks over to the coffee machine, where he picks up a Styrofoam cup. His back is to me as he pours the coffee. "What did I do that made you quit?"

I didn't expect him to speak, and the sound of his voice surprises me. "You didn't do anything. I quit baseball because of what I did to Laura. Or at least, because of what I thought I did."

"Laura?" he says, turning to face me. "I don't understand. What's Laura got to do with this?"

"Everything."

He sits down again, listening.

"I promised Laura I'd help her through her illness."

"What sort of illness? What are you talking about?"

"She was . . ." The words catch in my throat, and I have to swallow hard before I can choke them out. "She was emotionally ill."

"But she always seemed perfectly fine to me."

"To me, too, at least in the beginning. Then, when it all started, I promised her I'd stick by her. But I didn't. I've been punishing myself for leaving her ever since."

He sips his coffee and sits back in his chair. Outside the office I hear the sound of the chain drive closing the warehouse door.

"What do you mean by emotionally ill?" he asks.

"Laura is bipolar. I think she knew all along the chances were that she'd inherit it from her mother. That's why she never wanted much. Except for someone to love her."

My father leans forward and rests his elbows on the desk. "How come you never told your mother and me? Maybe we could've helped."

"Shame, I guess. I was ashamed of the way she looked in the hospital, of the way she acted, of what I thought she'd become. But most of all, I was ashamed of myself."

His eyes are fixed on mine, but he says nothing.

"I never meant to hurt you, Dad. I meant to hurt me. I didn't consider what my quitting would do to you. I was hoping that somehow you could understand. That you could forgive me."

He glances down at the coffee cup he holds in his heavy wrinkled hands, looking as if old age has fallen on him suddenly. I realize for the first time that his advancing years have made him vulnerable. Always before he seemed so intimidating. It's as if in this moment I have at last stepped out of his shadow; seen him in a new and totally different light.

"Does all this have something to do with why you went back to school and decided to work with retarded kids?"

"I think so. But they're not retarded, Dad. They have learning disabilities. It's different."

The office door opens and the mechanic says, "All locked up for the night, Carl. See you tomorrow." He shuts the door again, and I hear his footsteps echoing on the concrete floor.

"You and your brother were good kids," my father says, still looking at the cup in his hands. "Hardworking, dependable. But Rick never had your talent. When he gave up baseball, I was disappointed, but it didn't surprise me. I never really thought Rick could make it, even though he would've made a damn fine college catcher." He looks up at me. "But you. You could've made it." His voice is tinged with pride, nostalgia, and regret.

"I'm sorry I let you down."

"It wasn't me you let down. It was you."

"We should've talked about it then, Dad. I owed you that. But do you realize this is the first time in all the years that we've talked about anything besides sports? I mean really talked. Our whole relationship was built around baseball. How my arm felt, how I needed to keep practicing, how someday I'd get to the majors. I still remember that day in the hospital after Rick was hit in the head with the baseball. It was the only time I recall when we were really close to talking about something other than baseball. When I quit the game, we had nothing else to talk about."

He shifts in his chair.

My heart beats fast in my chest, as if I've just run a wind sprint. But I know I have to keep going, finish what I have to say.

"You go through your whole life with someone, and then one day they're gone and you've never told them how you feel. I don't want that to happen to us. I love you, Dad. And though you're hurt and disappointed that I walked away from the dream we shared, I know you still love me."

I look at him sitting in his chair, look into his eyes and wonder what he's thinking. And then I know. I know exactly what he's thinking.

I stand and walk to the door.

"Son," he says.

I stop and turn around. "Yes?"

He wets his lips, averts his eyes, and then he looks at me again. "I'm sorry about Laura. I wish I'd known her better. If I only would've known how much you loved her, we could've worked it out. You and me and your mother, we could've helped. You wouldn't have had to quit baseball." Tears well up in his eyes.

"I know that now, Dad."

He's holding back tears, trying hard not to let me see him cry.

"Maybe we can take in a Twins game."

"I'd like that."

"I'll see ya then, Dad."

He gives me a nod.

Epilogue

That summer I take a job at my father's warehouse, loading trucks. I'm tan and solid and filled out some, thanks to my mother's home cooking. In the evenings, to stay in shape, I drive over to the university and work out in the field house with the college ballplayers and my old coach, Paul Tatum.

After my workouts I shower and walk to the Wilson library on campus, where I'm doing research for a course I'm taking to keep my teaching certificate current. It might be too late for baseball, but it isn't too late to try teaching again—and someday I will.

One evening, I'm sitting at a table in the library reading an article on education from the latest Phi Delta Kappan journal when a familiar voice says, "Michael Collins."

I look up. Still scholarly and distinguished, Cameron Ford holds out his hand.

"What's it been?" he says. "Four years?"

I stand and shake his hand. "Closer to five, I think."

He nods in agreement. "Five it is. How have you been?"

"Fine."

"Still playing professional ball?"

"Not anymore."

"You're looking good. My God. The last time I saw you was, let's see . . ." He wrinkles his brow, trying to recall.

"It was at Laura's," I remind him. "You and your wife were over for dinner."

"Ah, yes. Laura's." He pauses, suddenly remembering, I assume, the night Laura came downstairs naked. His complexion darkens, and he gives me a half-smile.

I can't help thinking that the last time I saw *him*, he was in bed with Laura. I never confronted him about how he took advantage of her when he knew she was ill, and it seems pointless to confront him now, but hurt and anger simmer my blood and the heat rises in my face.

A strained silence envelops us, and as much as I want to ask him if he knows anything about her, I can tell our conversation has come to an uncomfortable end.

Finally, I say, "Good to see you again, Cameron."

He hesitates for a moment. Then he says, "Good to see you, too." He turns and starts off, stops, and turns around again. "I thought you might like to know."

I try to appear calm, but my heart feels as if it will burst my chest.

"About Laura," he says.

"Yes?"

"She's doing well, Michael. She lives north of here in Park Falls."

I tighten the grip on the pen in my hand.

"Monica corresponds with her. You remember my wife, Monica."

"Of course. How is she?"

"Still spending all her time on charity work," he replies with a shake of his head. He pauses again, contemplating.

I wonder if there is more he has to tell me. Uncertain if I want to hear it if there is, I wait.

At last he says, "Laura married a doctor. Nice fellow. David Gardner. A pediatrician, I believe. They have a child. A little girl. Laura is taking her prescribed medicine regularly and completing her doctorate. Getting control of her life again."

Though I try to hide it, Cameron must have seen the pain on my face because he says, "I'm sorry things didn't work out between you two." He stands there looking at me, and then he says again, "I'm sorry."

I nod.

"Take care, Michael." He starts to leave.

"Cameron?"

"Yes?"

"Thank you."

He smiles and walks away.

* * *

Whenever I think of autumn now, I think of it in terms of a beginning rather than an ending, of life rather than death. Maybe it's because the students are returning to school. Maybe it's the brilliant colors and the yellow leaves falling like meteors. Or maybe it's the crispness in the air that's so refreshing after summer's oppressive heat and humidity. Regardless, to me autumn means it's a time to be outdoors, to enjoy campfires and harvest moons, to savor nature's renaissance of colors. If ever there is a time to be in love, it's autumn.

I drive along Highway 47, a two-lane stretch of asphalt that runs like a dark ribbon through the sun-baked fields and small towns of northern Minnesota, towns with names like Bradford and Dalbo and Ogilvie. Weather-beaten houses and farms stand like outposts miles from the nearest neighbor. Not even the splash of fall colors, the red sumac, the yellow poplar, can wash away the feelings of loneliness and isolation that I sense out here. Perhaps I'm still too vulnerable for the solitude of the country.

It seems natural now to think of how things might have been, but those thoughts are only momentary, for I'm not intending to rekindle the past. I'm on my way to Park Falls because I need to get on with my life, to have some closure. And I know I can never have that till I see Laura one more time.

The drive north takes three hours. I'd purchased a used 2010 Chevy that ran well and probably could have made it in half the time had I chosen to take the interstate, but I'm in no hurry.

I feel more centered now, more secure than I have for the past five years. Beth Stanton was hired to replace Kate Fleming. I couldn't stay in Dakota Lake. Teaching is difficult enough without having to do so under a dark cloud, especially if the cloud was of my own making, and even if no one knew that but me. It was better for all concerned that I moved on, started anew, though no one ever starts completely fresh, for your past is like your shadow.

Yet, as dust settles over the pieces of my life, I can at last see clearly the direction I once took and the path I need to follow now in order to put my life back together again.

Nicole Stone put her house up for sale and moved back to Michigan. Detective Monroe stopped by my apartment one evening and told me that he'd worked out an agreement with the DA not to press charges against Danny O'Brien, as long as Danny and his family entered counseling. The family also agreed not to file a lawsuit against the school district or me. Late one night I received a phone call from Danny.

* * *

"I wanted to let you know I'm okay, Mr. C," he said. "They keep telling me in counseling that what happened was an accident."

"Believe them."

"I didn't get the scholarship, but I did make up my English grade. I'm going to the university to play hockey anyway."

"That's good news."

"My dad and me are getting along better, too. He even said he'd buy season tickets to the games."

"I'm glad to hear that, Danny."

"How about you, Mr. C? How are you getting along?"

"I'm okay."

"I heard you quit teaching."

"Yes," I said.

"Why? You really care about kids."

"I'll get back into it someday."

"I hope you do that. You will, won't you?"

"Yes, I will."

"Will you come to a hockey game this fall if I make the team?"

"You'll make it. And I'll be there to see you."

"I gotta go now. Is it all right if I call you again sometime?"

"Sure, Danny. Night or day. Anytime. You hang in there."

"Thanks, Mr. C," he said.

* * *

The sign welcoming me to Park Falls sets the population at 7,237. Main Street—the city council, though obviously good at math, apparently doesn't have much imagination—boasts a McDonald's and competing Burger King. I'm hungry and a little sleepy after the long drive, so I order at the Burger King drive-through and eat lunch in the car.

After I finish eating, I pull into a SuperAmerica station. As I fill the car's seemingly bottomless tank, I look for her. I always look for her. My adrenaline begins flowing when I see Dr. Gardner's address listed in the Park Falls phone book in the station. A pretty teenage girl behind the station's checkout counter gives me directions to the doctor's house.

I drive to the end of Main Street, past the hardware, drug, and grocery store, and turn right onto First Avenue, a curvy, two-lane tar road that follows a meandering stream. Though the day is clear and the sun bright, there's a noticeable drop in temperature between the city and here. I can already feel winter's chill.

Beyond the stream to my right lies a thick forest of birch and pine. The houses on my left are small, but set well back, allowing for large yards. Addresses are stickered on silver mailboxes along the side of the road. A strong pine smell scents the air. I pass a teenage boy and girl on horseback and a small, white, clapboard church with a steeple and a sign out front proclaiming JESUS SAVES.

A quarter mile past the church, on the outskirts of town, I see a shingle bearing the doctor's name attached to a mailbox. I park up the road and sit in my car, wondering what I'm going to do now that I'm here. I have been thinking all along that I'll be able to talk to Laura, but all of a sudden that doesn't seem like such a good idea. There's virtually no traffic, though I imagine that if I sit here too long, one of the local cops will cruise by or someone will call them.

It's peaceful. The driver's side window is open, and I listen to the water running over a rocky streambed, a woodpecker hammering on a trunk, sounds I often can't hear in the city.

I sit staring out the windshield for a while before I notice a gravel road in my rearview mirror that angles off to the left.

I start the car, back up, and turn onto the gravel road.

It follows a row of birch trees on my right and a picket fence on my left. The road runs parallel along the edge of the doctor's property for about a hundred yards before veering off to the right and into a small clearing in a public park. Four redwood picnic tables are placed near a circular barbecue pit. The pit is dug out of the ground and surrounded by smooth stones painted white. The whole area is studded with birch and pine trees.

I turn off the ignition and get out of the car. Through a clearing in the trees I can see the back of Laura's house about fifty yards away. The house is a rambling, two-story wooden structure with a screen porch, swing set, sandbox, and garden in the rear. Shades are drawn over the windows.

My heart picks up a beat as I maneuver closer to the house, weaving in and out of pine and birch trees, over brown grass that crunches like peanut shells under my feet. Ten yards short of the picket fence, I stop and lean against a pine tree. A light breeze ruffles my hair. I figure I'm about twenty-five yards from the house now.

While I wait, my mind replays a tape of the good times Laura and I spent together, simultaneously conjuring up images and dialogues of what it would be like to see and talk with her again.

I wait for an hour. My legs are stiff from standing in one spot for such a long time. I begin to think that this was a bad idea and that I should head back to the car and go home, when Laura comes out of the house.

It's such a shock to see her that I nearly cry out her name. I stand motionless, looking at her, remembering the first time we met on the plane to San Juan. It takes a moment to regain control, to realize that I can be seen.

I step behind a pine. When I catch my breath, I peer out from behind the tree. I can see her clearly, her brunette hair shoulder-length and shining in the sun. She wears a navy pea coat over a white turtleneck and jeans. I can see her face in profile; her smile as she bends down on one knee, claps her hands, and calls, "Michelle. Come on, Michelle."

In answer to her call a little dark-haired girl, dressed in a pink coat and mittens, comes running toward her in that wobbly, tentative kind of run small children have that makes them appear tipsy.

In that moment that Michelle runs into her mother's arms, I feel a sting of regret pass through me as I see myself standing alone in the cold at the end of Alexander Seaton's driveway. I wonder how different my life would be now if I'd had the courage to confront Seaton, the courage to deal with Laura's illness. Yet I also feel the weight of the past lifting. And as I wipe the tears from eyes, turn, and walk away, I know that I have seen Laura as she once was—as I always will remember her.

Made in the USA
Monee, IL
07 October 2020